The Three Investigators

in

The Mystery of the Stuttering Parrot

"Help!" The voice was weak and choked. "Please, someone—help me! Someone—quick, before I—"

Hearing the cries, Jupiter Jones and one of his partners burst into the gloomy old house. There on the floor lay a haggard man, bound and loosely gagged.

What in the world was going on? Jupiter's firm of young detectives had been called in to help this man find his lost parrot—an unusual bird that quoted Shakespeare with a stutter. But a lot more seemed to be at stake than a missing pet!

The Three Investigators

in

The Mystery of the Stuttering Parrot

By Robert Arthur

Random House *New York*

Originally published by Random House in 1964.
First Random House paperback edition, 1973.
Second Random House paperback edition, 1978.
Revised edition, 1985.

Library of Congress Cataloging in Publication Data:
Arthur, Robert.
  The Three Investigators in The mystery of the stuttering parrot.
  (The Three Investigators mystery series ; 2)
  Rev. ed. of: Alfred Hitchcock and The Three Investigators
in The mystery of the stuttering parrot. c1964.
  SUMMARY: In search of a lost parrot who recites
Shakespeare with a stutter, Jupiter Jones' firm of young
detectives becomes involved with a missing masterpiece.
  [1. Mystery and detective stories] I. Arthur, Robert.
Alfred Hitchcock and The Three Investigators in The
mystery of the stuttering parrot. II. Title. III. Series.
PZ7.A744Thfe 1985 [Fic] 83-26983
ISBN: 0-394-86402-6 (pbk.)

Manufactured in the United States of America
    3 4 5 6 7 8 9 0

Contents

Introduction by Hector Sebastian

Get set for another spine-chilling adventure with The Three Investigators. If you're already familiar with these three young detectives, don't waste any time and turn right to the story. But for everyone else, let me introduce the boys to you.

The three young men who call themselves The Three Investigators are Bob Andrews, Pete Crenshaw, and Jupiter Jones. They all live in the town of Rocky Beach, California, on the shore of the Pacific Ocean a few miles from Hollywood. Bob is slight, blond, loves books, and has a streak of real adventurousness in him. Pete is tall, muscular, and tends to be nervous before anything happens but is a source of great strength in any kind of trouble. Jupiter is the leader of the team. He's on the heavy side and has a mind like a steel trap. Though his round face can often show complete stupidity, there is in fact a shrewd, often penetrating mind working behind it.

Though Bob and Pete live with their parents, Jupiter lives with his aunt and uncle, since he was orphaned when he was very young. As a baby, Jupiter was precocious and adorable. He had a brief career as a child actor called Baby Fatso. Though Jupe's early acting experience often comes in handy when he's working on a case, he hates being called Baby Fatso or being reminded of that time.

In a contest sponsored by a local car rental agency, Jupiter won the use of a gold-plated vintage Rolls-Royce, complete with a chauffeur, for thirty days. With this transportation available to him—which is important in California, where distances are large—Jupiter and his two friends expanded the operations of The Three Investigators. Their motto is "We Investigate Anything" and they live up to that motto.

The Investigators' home base is The Jones Salvage Yard, a super junk yard run by Titus and Mathilda Jones, Jupiter's uncle and aunt. The boys' headquarters is an old thirty-foot trailer that they've stocked with an office, a darkroom, and a tiny laboratory. The trailer is hidden from view behind massive piles of junk and can be entered only through secret passageways the boys have built.

That's enough for now. Listen carefully, because some parrots are about to speak!

—HECTOR SEBASTIAN

The Three Investigators
in

The Mystery of the Stuttering Parrot

Chapter 1

A Cry for Help

"HELP!" The voice that called out was strangely shrill and muffled. "Help! Help!"

Each time a cry from within the mouldering old house pierced the silence, a new chill crawled down Pete Crenshaw's spine. Then the cries for help ended in a strange, dying gurgle and that was even worse.

The tall, brown-haired boy knelt behind the thick trunk of a barrel palm and peered up the winding gravel path at the house. He and his partner, Jupiter Jones, had been approaching it when the first cry had sent them diving into the shrubbery for cover.

Across the path, Jupiter, stocky and sturdily built, crouched behind a bush, also peering toward the house. They waited for further sounds. But now the old, Spanish-style house, set back in the neglected garden that had grown up like a small tropical jungle, was silent.

"Jupe!" Pete whispered. "Was that a man or a woman?"

Jupiter shook his head. "I don't know," he whispered back. "Maybe it was neither."

"Neither?" Pete gulped. It certainly hadn't been a child, and if it was neither a man nor a woman, that left only possibilities he didn't care to think about.

The two boys waited. The heat of a summer day in Hollywood was heavy and oppressive.

All around them were palm trees, bushes, and flowers gone wild. Once this land had been a lovely garden but years of neglect had turned it into a wilderness. The house beyond it was in disrepair, too.

It was the home of Malcolm Fentriss, a retired Shakespearean actor and a friend of Hector Sebastian, the detective turned mystery writer who had become the boys' mentor. Mr. Sebastian also sometimes found cases for them. In their capacity as investigators, the two boys had come to help Mr. Fentriss find a missing parrot. Mr. Sebastian had mentioned to them that the actor had lost his parrot and was very anxious to get it back.

Then had come the unexpected cry for help. Now they were crouched in the shrubbery, awaiting developments.

"Good grief!" Pete said in a low voice. "We started out to look for a missing parrot. Now before we even get to the house, someone is screaming for help! I hope this isn't going to be another case like the last one."

"On the contrary," his stocky partner whispered back, "it is starting very promisingly. But all seems quiet now. We'd better approach the house and find out what is happening."

"That isn't a house I want to approach," Pete told him. "It looks like a house full of locked rooms that shouldn't be opened."

"A very good description," Jupiter replied. "Remember to tell it to Bob when we get back to Headquarters."

Bob Andrews was the third member of the firm. He kept the records of their cases and did necessary research.

Jupiter started to slip toward the house, moving between bushes and flowers without stirring a ripple of movement in the vegetation. On the other side of the path, Pete kept abreast of him. They had come within a hundred feet of the house when something grabbed his ankle and he was flung to the ground. As he tried to pull free, the unseen hand gripped more tightly and jerked him back. Flat on his face, he couldn't see who or what had grabbed him.

"Jupe!" he gasped. "Something's got me!"

For all his stocky build, Jupiter moved swiftly. He darted across the path and was at Pete's side almost before the other boy finished speaking.

"What is it?" Pete croaked, rolling his eyes sideways at his partner. "Something's dragging me away. Is it a boa constrictor? This garden could hide anything."

Jupiter's round, determined features looked unusually grave.

"I'm sorry to tell you this, Pete," he said, "but you have been trapped by an unusually vicious specimen of *vitis vinifera*."

"Do something!" Pete gasped. "Don't let vitis whatever it is get me!"

"I have my knife," Jupiter said. "I'll do my best."

He whipped out his prized Swiss knife that had eight blades. Then he grasped Pete's leg. Pete could feel him slashing fiercely. The grip on his ankle relaxed. Pete immediately rolled away and sprang to his feet.

Behind him, his partner, with a broad grin, was putting away his knife. A heavy loop of vine that had been cut in the middle was bobbing up and down close to the ground.

"You put your foot into a twisted grapevine," Jupiter said. "The harder you pulled to get away, the harder the vine pulled you back. It was a very evenly matched test. Neither of you was using any intelligence. The vine doesn't have any, and you allowed panic to cloud your mental processes."

Jupiter usually talked like that. By now Pete was used to it.

"Okay, okay," Pete said sheepishly. "I panicked. I was thinking about that call for help, I guess."

"Panic is more dangerous than danger itself," Jupiter said. "Fear robs the individual of the ability to make proper decisions. It destroys—destroys—— Ulp!"

Looking at Jupiter, Pete had the impression that his partner was displaying all the symptoms of the fear he had just been talking about. He had suddenly turned pale. His eyes bulged. His jaw dropped. He seemed to be looking at something just behind Pete's back.

"You're a good actor, Jupe," Pete said. "That's the best imitation of fright I've ever seen. But now what do you say we—we——"

He turned and he saw what Jupiter was looking at. And the words stuck in his throat.

Jupiter was not acting. The very fat man who stood

facing them, with a large, old-fashioned pistol in his hand, would have startled anybody.

The fat man wore glasses that magnified his eyes into great round orbs like the eyes of some huge fish in an aquarium. The sunlight glinted on the glasses and made the eyes behind them seem to throw out flashes of fire.

"All right, boys!" the fat man said. He gave the pistol a wave. "Into the house with you. Then we'll find out what mischief you are up to. Now, march!"

With dragging footsteps and dry mouths, Pete and Jupiter trudged ahead of him up the gravel path to the somber, decaying old house.

"Don't try to run, boys!" the fat man warned. "Or you'll wish you hadn't."

"Don't run, Pete," Jupiter whispered. "That would be the worst thing possible. We want to convince Mr. Fentriss we are here on legitimate business."

"I'm not going to run," Pete whispered back. "My legs are so wobbly, I feel as if I were just learning to walk."

Their feet scrunched on the gravel. Behind them the fat man's greater weight made the gravel crunch with a sound that gave Pete a very crawly feeling. He was almost glad when they stepped on the tiled patio of the house and paused before the huge front door.

"Now open the door, boys," the fat man said. "Step inside. Remember that I have an itchy trigger finger. Turn to your right. Enter the room there, and take seats against the far wall."

Jupiter turned the knob. The door swung open, revealing a dark hall. Pete braced himself and they both stepped in, turned right, and entered a large room cluttered with books and newspapers and old furniture. Against the opposite wall were several very large leather chairs. They marched across the room and sat down.

The fat man stood looking at them with satisfaction. He blew into the barrel of his pistol, as if removing a speck of dust that might get in the way of a bullet.

"Now," he said, "you had better explain what mischief you had in mind, slipping so sneakily up to my house through my garden."

"We were just coming to call on you, Mr. Fentriss," Jupiter said. "You see——"

But the fat man did not let him finish. He put his finger alongside his nose and looked slyly at them.

"Just coming to call?" he asked. "Slipping from tree to tree, like thieves? Or cutthroats?"

"We heard somebody yell for help," Pete blurted out. "When that happened we ducked behind the trees to see what was happening."

"Ah." The fat man pursed his lips. "You heard that, did you? Someone calling for help?"

"You see," Jupiter explained, "Mr. Hector Sebastian, the famous mystery novelist, sent us here. He said you had lost your parrot and the police wouldn't help you find it. We're investigators, and we were coming to assist you in the recovery of your missing pet."

He reached into his pocket and produced one of their business cards, on which was printed:

THE THREE INVESTIGATORS

"We Investigate Anything"

? ? ?

First Investigator: Jupiter Jones
Second Investigator: Peter Crenshaw
Records and Research: Bob Andrews

"I'm Jupiter Jones," Jupiter said. "This is my partner, Pete Crenshaw."

"Oh." The fat man took the card and studied it. "Investigators, eh? And what are the question marks for? Do you doubt your ability?"

Pete had been waiting for that question. Practically everybody asked about those question marks. Jupiter had dreamed them up in a burst of inspiration. They were terrific for getting people interested.

"The question mark, otherwise known as the interrogation mark," Jupiter said, "stands for things unknown, questions unanswered, riddles unravelled. Our business is answering the questions, unravelling the riddles, investigating any mysteries that may come our way. Hence, the question mark is the symbol of The Three Investigators."

"I see, I see," Mr. Fentriss replied, slipping the card into his pocket. "And you were coming to investigate the mystery of my missing parrot. Ah."

He smiled at them. For the first time Pete's spirits rose. And then, at his next words, Pete's spirits sank deeper than ever.

"I wish I could believe that. You're such likely lads,

I'm sure your families are going to miss you," the fat man said.

Very deliberately he took a cigar from his pocket and clamped it between his teeth. Then he leveled the pistol at them and pulled the trigger.

There was a loud click. A bright blue flame appeared at the muzzle of the pistol. Mr. Fentriss held the flame to his cigar, took a deep puff to light it, then blew out the flame and put the pistol down on a table.

Gee, Pete thought, a cigar lighter! And all of his blood, which for that awful moment seemed to be drained out of him, came back and started to circulate again.

"Congratulations, boys!" Mr. Fentriss said jovially. "You passed the test with flying colors. In the face of my efforts to intimidate you, you held firm! Let me shake your hands."

He strode over and shook their hands. The grip of his pudgy hand was terrific. He chuckled as he helped them to their feet.

"I'm proud of you," he said. "Many a grown man would have quailed in the face of my hostility. I shall have to telephone my friend Hector to tell him that you withstood my little test very well."

"Your . . . little . . . test?" Jupiter said deliberately. It seemed the First Investigator was having some trouble speaking as calmly as usual. "You mean you knew who we were the whole time?"

"Exactly," Mr. Fentriss said. "Hector telephoned me to let me know you were coming and I decided to give you a little surprise to test your mettle. So many people claim to be heroes these days. And you have indeed displayed rare courage. I'm only sorry I have no case for you to investigate."

"Then," Pete said, "your parrot isn't missing? But Mr. Sebastian said you were all broken up about it."

"Oh, it was missing, it was missing," Mr. Fentriss said. "And indeed, I was inconsolable. But it came back. Just this morning it flew back in the window I kept open for it. Dear Billy, what a worry he gave me."

"Billy?" Jupiter asked. "Is that the parrot's name?"

"That's right. Billy Shakespeare, short for William Shakespeare."

"But what about the call for help?" Pete asked. "It came from this house, and . . . well . . ."

"You were suspicious. Naturally," Mr. Fentriss boomed. "But that was Billy. The naughty rascal is something of an actor himself. I taught him to pretend he was in jail—behind bars in his cage, you know—and he amuses himself by calling for help."

"Could we see Billy?" Jupiter asked. "He must be a very talented bird."

"I'm sorry." Mr. Fentriss' face clouded. "Billy was making such a nuisance of himself that just as you arrived I put the cloth over his cage. That quiets him, you know. If I were to take it off now, he would start up again."

"Well, in that case I guess there's nothing to investigate," Jupiter said, sounding disappointed. "We'll be going, Mr. Fentriss. Anyway, I'm glad your parrot came back."

"Thank you, my boy," the stout man said. "And I shall keep your card. Any time I do have a mystery that needs investigation, I shall notify The Three Investigators."

He showed the two boys to the door. Pete and Jupiter started down the winding path that went through the tangled garden.

"I must confess to being disappointed," Jupiter said. "The case began most promisingly. A lonely house, a cry for help, a sinister fat man . . . I had high hopes."

"The opinions expressed are not necessarily those of the Second Investigator," Pete said. "Personally, I'm satisfied just to hunt for a missing parrot. I don't need any calls for help or sinister fat men. Let's work up gradually to all that."

"Perhaps you're right," Jupiter said, but he didn't sound as if he really meant it.

In silence they continued on to the street. It was a winding street in a rather old and run-down section of Hollywood, where big old houses, far apart, were slowly going to seed because the owners could not afford to take care of them.

At the curb was a Rolls-Royce with gold-plated fittings. As a prize for winning a contest, Jupiter was allowed the use of this handsome car, complete with Worthington, an English chauffeur, for thirty days.

"I guess we'd better go home, Worthington," Jupiter said as he and Pete climbed into the back of the old but luxurious car. "The parrot came back of its own accord."

"Very good, Master Jones," Worthington replied in a crisp British accent.

He pulled the car forward and maneuvered it to turn around. As he did so, Jupiter stared out the window at the garden of Mr. Fentriss' home—the house itself was hidden from sight behind palm trees and flowering bushes.

"Pete," he said abruptly, "please examine the scene carefully. Something is wrong, but I cannot detect what."

"What scene?" Pete asked. "You mean the garden?"

"The garden, the driveway, the entire grounds. I have a distinct sense of wrongness, yet the source of it eludes me."

"You mean something doesn't add up and you can't figure out what?"

Jupiter nodded, pinching his lower lip, always a sign that his mental machinery was moving into high gear.

Pete surveyed the whole area of grounds and garden. He couldn't see anything wrong, except that it needed a gardener working day and night for a month to make it look tidy. There was a driveway with a lot of fallen palm fronds on it. A car had recently gone up the driveway, squashing many of the palm leaves, but that didn't mean anything.

"I don't see a thing," he reported. Jupiter didn't seem to hear him. He was staring out the rear window as they drove away, still pinching his lower lip, thinking furiously.

They had gone almost ten blocks when suddenly Jupiter whirled around.

"Worthington!" he cried. "We have to go back. Fast!"

"Very good, Master Jones." The chauffeur deftly wheeled the big car around. "Go back it shall be."

"Hey, Jupe!" Pete protested. "What bit you? Why are we going back?"

"Because now I know what was wrong," Jupiter said, his round face flushed with excitement. "There are no telephone wires leading into Mr. Fentriss' house."

"No telephone wires?" Pete tried to figure out what his partner was getting at.

"Light wires, yes, but no telephone wires," Jupiter said.

"And Mr. Fentriss distinctly stated that Mr. Sebastian had telephoned him we were coming. That was a lie. If that was a lie, probably everything else he told us was a lie."

"A lie?" Pete shook his head. "Why would he lie?"

"Because he isn't Mr. Fentriss!" Jupiter said. "He's an imposter. That was Mr. Fentriss we heard calling for help!"

Chapter 2

The Stuttering Parrot

THE BIG ROLLS-ROYCE raced down the winding street. When they had covered nine blocks, Pete and Jupiter saw a small, black foreign car pull out of a driveway ahead and turn toward them. It picked up speed swiftly and raced past them. They just had time to see the figure of the man at the wheel.

The driver was a very fat man, wearing large glasses. They couldn't see his face well because it was turned away from them.

"That's Mr. Fentriss!" Pete shouted.

"Correction. It's the man who pretended to be Mr. Fentriss," Jupiter said. "Don't let him get away, Worthington! Follow to see where he is going."

"Right, Master Jones," the chauffeur said, and put on the brakes. He started to turn around. Pete looked doubtfully after the fast-vanishing foreign car.

"What can we do if we catch him?" he asked. "We haven't any evidence against him. Besides, the real Mr. Fentriss may need our help."

Jupiter hesitated, torn between a desire to follow the

fleeing imposter and a desire to help someone who might need their aid. Then he nodded.

"You're right," he said. "First we must discover if Mr. Fentriss is unharmed. Continue to Mr. Fentriss' home," he requested of Worthington.

The chauffeur continued on up the street until they reached Mr. Fentriss' driveway, from which the foreign car had emerged. Worthington turned into it and eased the big car along the narrow road, past palm trees and bushes which brushed its sides, until they came to the rear of the old house in which Pete and Jupiter had been a few moments earlier.

"Pete," Jupiter said, quietly. "Tell me—the foreign car that passed us—did you notice anything about it?"

"It was a two-door sports model Ranger, a very good English car," Pete said. "Practically new. It had a California license plate. I didn't get the number except I remember it ended in 13."

"Did you get the license number, Worthington?" Jupiter asked.

"I'm sorry, Master Jones," the chauffeur answered. "I was intent on the road and failed to observe the car closely. I did note that it was a Ranger, however, and had red leather upholstery."

"Well, we know something. Later we will tackle the job of finding the fat man and his car again," Jupiter said, hopping out of the Rolls. "Now let's see if the real Mr. Fentriss is within."

Following him, Pete couldn't help wondering how

Jupiter was going to find one single car out of the millions of cars in Southern California. But somehow he had a notion Jupiter would find a way.

Then Pete and his stocky partner paused abruptly. From the gloomy old house came another cry for help.

"Help!" the voice was weak and choked. "Please, someone—help me. Someone—quick, before I——"

The voice trailed off into nothing.

"He sounds as if he's dying!" Pete gasped. "Come on!"

With his long legs he led the way to the back door. It stood slightly open as if the fat man had left it that way in his haste to leave. They entered, blinking as their eyes adjusted to the dimmer light.

For a moment they stood listening. No sound broke the silence, except the faint creak of an old board.

"We were in that room," Jupiter said, pointing down the hall. "We'd better try the opposite side of the house."

They hurried down the hall and tried the door on their right. It opened into a big, old-fashioned living room which had a huge bay window.

"Who's—there?" It was a weak voice, and it seemed to come from a large plant in the bay window. A purple flower bobbed up and down and Pete had the strange sensation that the flower was talking to them.

"Has—someone come?" the flower seemed to ask. Then Pete saw something huddled behind the tub in which the flower was rooted, almost hidden by trailing leaves.

"This way!" Pete cried. In a few strides he was kneeling beside a very haggard, rather thin man who lay on his side, hands and feet bound, a cloth rudely tied between his teeth.

"It's all right, Mr. Fentriss," he said. "We'll untie you."

The knots proved quite loose and were quickly removed. The gag Mr. Fentriss had already almost worked from his mouth. Leaning on Pete and Jupiter, he managed to reach a leather couch, where he stretched out.

"Thank you, boys," he whispered. "I'll get my strength back in a minute."

Jupiter, looking solemn, pulled up a chair and sat down.

"Mr. Fentriss," he said, "I think we should call the police."

The man looked alarmed. "No, no!" he said. "Anyway, we can't. I have no telephone."

"We can call from the car, sir. We have a mobile phone."

"No," Mr. Fentriss insisted. "However . . ." He rolled over and leaned on his elbow to stare at the stocky boy. "Who are you? How do you happen to be here?"

Jupiter handed him one of The Three Investigators' business cards and explained how Hector Sebastian had sent them.

"That was very nice of Hector," Mr. Fentriss said.

"Are you sure you don't want us to call the police?" Jupiter asked. "Naturally, if you wish us to try to recover your parrot, The Three Investigators are at your service. However, you have been assaulted and bound and——"

"No!" Mr. Fentriss said. "I will be very happy to have

you boys undertake the case for me. I feel I can trust you. I have already been to the police. At first they said my parrot probably flew away. Then, when I became insistent, they hinted that since I am an actor I was seeking publicity."

"I understand, sir," Jupiter said. "They might think this was still another attempt at publicity."

"Yes, my boy." Mr. Fentriss relaxed. "Therefore—no police. You must promise."

They promised, and Jupiter requested all the facts concerning the missing parrot.

"I was very attached to Billy," the man said. "His full name is Billy Shakespeare. You know who William Shakespeare was, of course."

"Yes, sir," Jupiter said. "The world's greatest playwright. Born in England in 1564 and died in 1616. His plays are still popular all over the world. *Hamlet* is probably his best-known play."

"Many's the time I played Hamlet," Mr. Fentriss said with animation. "Oh, I was a great success as Hamlet." He put one hand against his chest and stretched out his other hand. In a deep voice, he said, " 'To be, or not to be, that is the question.' " Then he turned to the boys. "A line from *Hamlet*," he said. "Probably the best-known line Shakespeare ever wrote. And my parrot used to quote it. He said it over and over."

"Your parrot quoted Shakespeare?" Pete asked. "He must have been a very educated bird."

"He was, definitely. He quoted it in a very good British accent. There was only one drawback."

"Drawback?" Jupiter asked.

"The poor bird stuttered," Mr. Fentriss told him. "When he quoted the line, he said, 'To-to-to be or not to-to-to be, that is the question.' "

Jupiter's eyes lighted with intense interest.

"Did you hear that, Pete?" he asked. "Who ever heard of a stuttering parrot before? I have a feeling that this is going to be a most unusual case."

Pete had a feeling, too. He had a strange, sinking feeling that Jupe was right.

As Mr. Fentriss regained his strength, Jupiter proceeded to get the facts from him. The actor had owned his stuttering parrot about three weeks. He had bought it from a peddler, a small man with a strong Mexican accent who had driven up to the house in a little Mexican donkey cart.

"We must have all the facts, sir," Jupiter said. "How did this peddler happen to come to your house?"

"Oh, Miss Irma Waggoner sent him," the man said. "She lives in the next block. She bought a parrot from him, and when she heard Billy quote Shakespeare, she felt sure I would be interested. So she sent him here."

"I see." Jupiter was pinching his lower lip. "Was this man a regular parrot peddler?"

"Why, I really don't know." Mr. Fentriss blinked vaguely. "When I saw him he had just two cages on his cart. One held Billy. The other held some curious-looking darkish bird, all bedraggled, which, he said, was a rare black parrot. But I was sure no such thing existed. He said no one would buy it because it looked ill."

"Did he tell you his name or have any name written on his car?"

"No." The actor shook his head. "He was raggedly dressed, and he coughed badly, and he seemed very anxious to sell the parrot. I bought it for only fifteen dollars. You see, no one else had been willing to buy it because it stuttered."

"And it was just a plain, two-wheeled donkey cart?" Jupiter asked.

"That's right," Mr. Fentriss agreed. "Badly needing paint. It was pulled by a little donkey he called Pablo, but that's all I can tell you."

"You think he stole the parrots, Jupe?" Pete asked.

"I doubt that he would have been selling them on the open street if he had," Jupiter said thoughtfully. "However, it is obvious that he was not the original owner and trainer of Billy."

"How do you figure that?"

"Quite simply. Mr. Fentriss says Billy spoke with a British accent. The man who sold it had a Mexican accent."

"Oh, sure." Pete could have kicked himself for missing that one.

"Now, Mr. Fentriss," Jupiter said to the tall man, who was sitting up, "tell me all you can about the disappearance of the parrot."

"Well, my boy," Mr. Fentriss answered, "about three days ago I went for an evening stroll. I left the door unlocked and the window open. When I returned, Billy was gone. There were tire tracks in my driveway, and I don't own a car. To me it was obvious that someone had driven up, entered the house, and stolen Billy in my absence.

"And the police said he flew away!" The actor's voice grew deep with scorn. "Have you ever heard of a parrot flying away and taking his cage with him?"

"No, sir," Jupiter agreed. "Now that we have the background facts, please tell us all you can about what happened today. That is, about the fat man and what he wanted and how he came to tie you up."

"That scoundrel!" the actor exclaimed. "First he told me his name was Claudius, and that he was from the police. They had sent him to help me find my lost parrot. He asked more or less the same questions you did, and I gave him the same answers. Then he asked me if I knew anyone else in the neighborhood who had bought a parrot from the Mexican peddler, and I mentioned Miss Waggoner.

"That seemed to interest him very much. Next he asked me what my parrot said when it spoke, and I told him I had already reported that to the police. This seemed to confuse him, but he replied he merely wanted to check, so I told him that Billy always said, 'My name is Billy Shakespeare. To be or not to be, that is the question.'

"At this he grew even more excited, and wrote the speech down carefully."

"Excuse me, Mr. Fentriss," Pete put in. "You didn't tell him that Billy stuttered?"

"No." The actor passed his hand across his forehead.

"I was afraid the police would simply laugh at the idea of a stuttering parrot."

"Yet Mr. Claudius was very interested in the bird's speech," Jupiter said. "Can you tell us anything more, sir?"

"I don't believe so." The actor shook his head. "Oh, yes, one strange thing. This man, Mr. Claudius, asked me if the peddler had had any other parrots for sale. I mentioned the dark bird that seemed ill, and he became tremendously excited.

" 'That must be Blackbeard,' he said out loud. 'Yes, that certainly must be Blackbeard.' At that point I became very suspicious. I became convinced that Mr. Claudius was not from the police at all."

"Excuse me, Mr. Fentriss." Jupiter looked at the notes he had been making. "I forgot to ask for a description of your parrot," he said. "What type of parrot it is. You know, there are many varieties."

"I know nothing of such things," Mr. Fentriss said. "However, Billy has a beautiful yellow head and chest."

"Now, Mr. Fentriss, what happened when the fat man, Mr. Claudius, saw you were suspicious of him?"

"Why, I confronted him," the actor said indignantly. He drew himself up to his full height. Like an actor on the stage, he stretched out his hand. " 'You are not from the police!' " he said in a deep, dramatic voice, " 'I believe you are the infernal scoundrel who stole my Billy. Return him at once or it will be the worse for you.' That's what I said."

"And then?" Jupiter asked.

"And then," said Mr. Fentriss, "we heard a noise outside. Mr. Claudius rushed to the window. Apparently he saw you boys coming up the walk, and he may have thought police were with you. He swiftly overpowered me. I called for help, but he bound me, gagged me, and hurried out. After that I lay here until you rescued me.

"I don't understand it at all," he said. "But I do want Billy back. Do you think you can possibly find him for me?"

"The Three Investigators," Jupiter said, "will do their best."

Then, having all the information they could get, they said good-bye and Jupiter led Pete back out to the car. Worthington was polishing it, but he ceased as they appeared.

"Home, Master Jones?" he asked as they clambered in.

"I guess so," Jupiter agreed. As they started out the long, winding drive, he turned to Pete.

"I think it is almost certain," he said, "that Mr. Claudius stole Billy Shakespeare. He came back because he needed more information. Our first job, then, is to locate Mr. Claudius."

"I'd rather not," Pete said. "He looked like a man who could use a real pistol just as easily as he used that cigar lighter. Anyway, how can you find him without any clues at all?"

"I will ponder the problem," Jupiter said. "There must be some way—— Worthington, look out!"

His warning was not needed. The chauffeur had already seen the new gray sedan racing into the driveway directly toward them and had turned the wheel hard. The Rolls-Royce ploughed into an old, neglected flower bed while the oncoming sedan shrieked to a stop, brakes locked, tires skidding, as the small, sharp-eyed man at the wheel fought to avoid a collision.

Chapter 3

Little Bo-Peep Is Lost

THE TWO CARS stopped, the fender of the sedan barely an inch from the gleaming paintwork of the fine old Rolls-Royce. Worthington descended from the driver's seat with speed but dignity, and confronted the small, sharp-eyed man who came charging out of the front seat of the sedan.

"Why don't you watch where you're going, you big ape?" the small man shouted at him. Worthington drew himself up to his full six feet two.

"My man," he said, "I was leaving the premises at a moderate speed. You were racing in here recklessly. If you had damaged this car, it would have gone hard with you."

Worthington sounded as if he meant every word he said, and the smaller man, dressed in new, flashy clothing, fell back a step.

"Watch yourself!" he growled. "I don't take lip from servants."

"Do not," Worthington said, "call me a servant. Or I shall chastise you properly."

He reached out as if to take the small man by the lapels of his coat and shake him. The other hastily darted a hand in under his jacket. At that moment the rear door of the sedan opened and a big man, very expensively dressed, stepped out.

"Adams!" he said. "Get back into the car!"

His voice was crisp and commanding. He had a slight French accent, wore a narrow black moustache, and had a small mole at the corner of his mouth.

The driver hesitated, then, scowling, got back into the car, where a third man, large and ugly, sat watching. The man who had emerged from the car came forward.

"I am sorry," he said to Worthington, "that my driver was so careless. Fortunately, this wonderful car was not struck. I could not have forgiven myself if I had damaged such a car. Now, may I speak to your master?"

Up to this point events had moved too rapidly for Jupiter and Pete to take any action. But now Jupiter emerged from the car.

"You wanted to speak to me?" he asked.

The man looked surprised.

"You—ah—you are the owner of this Rolls-Royce?" he asked.

"It is mine for the moment." Jupiter's voice was off-hand. Because of his childhood acting experience, he could appear well poised in almost any situation. "I may make a change later."

"I see." The man hesitated. "May I ask—are you a friend of Mr. Fentriss, whom I was coming to call on?"

"I believe I can say we are friends, yes," Jupiter said,

and Pete, watching, had to admire his partner's air of nonchalance. Jupe certainly knew how to talk to adults when he had to. "We have just been calling on him."

"Then perhaps you can tell me," the man said, "how his parrot, Billy Shakespeare, is."

"Still missing," Jupiter said. "Mr. Fentriss is very despondent about it."

"Missing!" The man's face revealed nothing. "I'm sorry to hear that. No sign of it, I suppose?"

"No sign whatever," Jupiter said. "We are on our way to the police to ask what progress they have made. Shall we tell them you are interested in helping find it?"

"Oh, no, no," the man said quickly, seeming alarmed at the mention of the word police. "No need to mention me to them. I'm just a friend who stopped by to ask about Billy. But since he's still missing, I won't even bother Mr. Fentriss. I do hope he gets the bird back, but at the moment I think we will be on our way."

Without giving his name, the well-dressed man with the French accent climbed back into the car.

"Adams!" he said sharply. "Take me back to the hotel."

"Yes, sir," the sharp-eyed driver grumbled. He gave Worthington an ugly look, backed the sedan out of the driveway, and in a moment car and men were gone.

"You handled the situation very well, sir," Worthington said, as Jupiter got back into the car. "May I say that I was proud of you?"

"Thank you, Worthington," Jupiter said.

"Look," Pete demanded, "may I ask what that was all

about? Those men in that car were tough customers. I mean, the kind I'd hate to meet in a dark alley. How did you scare them off?"

Jupiter let out a deep breath and slumped back into his normal, somewhat stocky, boyish appearance again.

"It was a bluff," he said. "I gambled that the mention of the police would alarm them, so I falsely said we were going there."

"Sure," Pete agreed, as Worthington backed the car into the driveway and eased it out to the street again, "I saw that. But——"

"That driver, the one called Adams, probably carried a weapon," Jupiter said. "In a shoulder holster. Didn't you see him start to reach for it? Obviously he is a character used to violence."

"A weapon, huh? And used to using it?" Pete gulped.

"His employer restrained him," Jupiter said. "His employer is a man of much higher type. I wonder why he should want a gunman driving his car?"

"What I wonder," Pete said, as the car rolled down the street, "is why we have to get mixed up with such characters. All we started out to do was find a lost parrot."

"True," Jupiter agreed.

"So far we've run into a sinister fat man, a man with a foreign accent who has a hired thug driving his car, and heard about a mysterious Mexican peddler. And all of them are interested in the same bird."

"All but the peddler," Jupiter corrected. "Having sold the bird, his interest no longer exists."

"But why?" Pete asked, bewildered. "What is there

about a stuttering parrot that makes these rough characters seem to want it even if they have to steal it?"

"In the course of time," Jupiter said, "I have no doubt
that our investigation will reveal the answer. At the
moment, I am in a state of total bewilderment."

"Well, at least we're in the same state," Pete grumbled.
"If you want to know what I think———"

"What is it, Worthington?" Jupiter interrupted to ask.

"Someone in the road, Master Jones," the chauffeur
answered. "A lady who seems to have lost something."

The boys looked out. Turning a corner, Worthington
had jammed on the brakes, bringing the car to an abrupt
stop.

A small, plump woman was standing in the road, quite
oblivious to traffic, peering into the bushes and calling,
"Here, Pretty, Pretty. Come to Irma. I have some nice
sunflower seeds for you."

"Someone in difficulty," Jupiter said. "We'd better see
if we can help."

They got out of the car and approached the woman,
who was still peering up into the thick bushes along the
street and holding out a sunflower seed hopefully.

"Excuse me," Jupiter said, "have you lost something?"

"Why, yes, I have," the woman said. As she spoke she
tilted her head to one side, quite like a bird, and spoke in
a birdlike voice. "Little Bo-Peep is lost, and I don't know
where to find her.

"You haven't seen her, have you?" the woman asked.
"You haven't seen Little Bo-Peep?"

"No, ma'am," Jupiter said. "Little Bo-Peep is a parrot?"

"Why, yes." The woman looked at him in surprise. "How on earth did you know?"

Jupiter whipped out one of their business cards.

"We're investigators," he said. "I deduced that you were looking for a parrot because you have put a parrot cage on the grass near the edge of those shrubs, and because you are trying to entice the bird with sunflower seeds, of which parrots are very fond."

Well, Pete had figured that much, but the woman seemed to find it very remarkable. After exclaiming a few times, she asked them to come into her house to talk about the strange disappearance of Little Bo-Peep.

"Wait for us, Worthington," Jupiter called to the chauffeur, and he and Pete accompanied the small woman up a brick path to a bungalow hidden behind a screen of banana trees.

When they had seated themselves in the small living room, Jupiter asked, "Did you buy Little Bo-Peep a few weeks ago from a peddler with a strong Mexican accent, Miss Waggoner?"

"Why, yes," Miss Waggoner said, her eyes wide. "You know that and my name, too. You must be very good detectives."

"It's merely a matter of putting together information, Miss Waggoner," Jupiter said. "Mr. Fentriss mentioned a Miss Irma Waggoner, and you were calling to Bo-Peep to come to Irma, so you see I had all the facts necessary."

"Many people have facts," Miss Waggoner said, "and never learn how to put them together properly. Having facts is only part of the job. But don't tell me poor Mr. Fentriss still hasn't found Billy?"

"No, ma'am. Billy is still missing," Pete said. "We are trying to find him. Can you tell us just how your parrot happened to vanish?"

"Why, I just took a walk down to the store," Miss Waggoner said. "Little Bo-Peep was out of sunflower seeds and she does love them so. As I started out I was almost run down by a small, black foreign car coming around the corner. Goodness, how people drive these days!"

Pete and Jupiter exchanged glances. Neither of them had missed her reference to the small, black foreign car, and they both had the same thought. When last seen, Mr. Claudius had been driving in this direction.

"Well," Miss Waggoner went on, "I continued on to the store and bought the sunflower seeds. I strolled a bit on the way back, enjoying the sunshine, and when I entered the house I found the door of Bo-Peep's cage wide open and my little darling gone. I assumed I had left the cage open and she had flown out and might be in the yard someplace. I was hunting for her when you came along."

"The car that almost knocked you down, Miss Waggoner," Jupiter said. "Did you see it again?"

"Oh, no." She shook her head. "It turned the corner up the block and disappeared behind all those trees and bushes up there. My goodness, you don't suppose that fat man driving it stole Bo-Peep, do you?"

"I'm very much afraid he did," Jupiter told her. "We think he also stole Mr. Fentriss' Billy."

"Oh, my goodness!" Miss Waggoner said helplessly. "What a heartless man! But why would he go to so much trouble to get some parrots? He could buy his own."

That was what Pete would have liked to know. But Jupiter didn't have any answer to the question.

"So far it is a mystery," he said. "Did Little Bo-Peep talk, Miss Waggoner?"

"Oh, she certainly did. She said, 'Little Bo-Peep has lost her sheep and doesn't know where to find it. Call on Sherlock Holmes.' Isn't that a curious speech to teach a parrot?"

"Yes, ma'am," Jupiter agreed. "Did she say this in a British accent?"

"Yes, a very cultivated British accent, as if she had been carefully taught by a well-educated Englishman."

Jupiter scribbled all this down for Bob Andrews, who kept all the records of their cases.

"Miss Waggoner," he said when he had finished, "I feel sure the fat man who calls himself Mr. Claudius slipped into your house in your absence and stole Little Bo-Peep. You should call the police."

"The police? Oh, my goodness, no!" Miss Waggoner said. "It would mean going all the way downtown to tell them about it and—oh, no, you must help me! Please say you will," she begged, looking very flustered and upset.

"Very well, Miss Waggoner," Jupiter said. "As I am sure Mr. Claudius has both parrots, we can conduct both investigations at the same time."

"Oh, I'm so grateful to you. You've made me feel better already."

"One more question," Jupiter said. "You bought Little Bo-Peep from a Mexican peddler driving a two-wheeled donkey cart?"

"Yes. He was coughing badly and seemed ill. I was sorry for him."

"Did he give you a receipt or a bill of sale for the parrot?"

"Why, no." Miss Waggoner looked blank. "I never thought to ask."

"You didn't notice any name or address written on the donkey cart?" Jupiter persisted, but Miss Waggoner shook her head. She couldn't tell them a thing more.

Since there apparently weren't any more clues, the boys bade Miss Waggoner a polite good-bye and left. As soon as they got outside, Pete grabbed his stocky partner's arm.

"Jupe," he said, "will you tell me how you expect to find two parrots named Billy Shakespeare and Little Bo-Peep, who could be anyplace by now? I admit they may be very literary parrots, who know Shakespeare and *Mother Goose*, but there must be millions of parrots back in the jungle to take their place. We're wasting our time."

Jupiter looked thoughtful.

"Did you think Mr. Claudius was a frivolous type of individual?" he asked.

"Well, no," Pete admitted. "When he pointed that pistol at us I thought he was more of a brutal kind of individual."

"Exactly. Yet he has gone to much trouble to steal two

parrots with peculiar names and unusual abilities. His reasons we cannot yet deduce. But we must assume they are excellent reasons, must we not?"

"I suppose so," Pete grumbled. "But how much chance have we of ever finding him again?"

"We are investigators. We have intelligence," Jupiter said. The determined look on his face told his partner that nothing was going to change his mind. "In addition——Look out!"

He flung himself against Pete, and they went down together in a tangle of arms and legs. Something large and solid whizzed by the place Pete's head had been a moment before, and plowed into the soft turf.

"Get—get off me!" Pete gasped, all his breath gone, for Jupiter had fallen directly on his stomach. "I can't—breathe. I can't—move."

Jupiter scrambled up, and Pete drew a deep breath. Slowly he got to his feet, as his partner pulled the object from the grass. It was a piece of red clay tiling, like the red tiles on the roof of Miss Waggoner's bungalow.

"If that had hit either of us," Jupiter said, "it would have incapacitated us for a long time. Fortunately I saw a movement in the bushes just before it came sailing toward us."

"Th-thanks," Pete said shakily. "Who threw it?"

"I did not observe the one who threw it. However, I feel sure it was meant as a warning. Someone does not want us to look for Billy Shakespeare or Little Bo-Peep!"

Chapter 4

Red Gate Rover

BOB ANDREWS was eating his supper, in between glances at the telephone. He had been expecting it to ring any minute, ever since he got home from the library. He worked there part time, helping return books to the shelves and doing other similar jobs.

But he was on dessert now—baked cup custard with a nice brown crust on top—and though he was scraping the last speck from the side of his dish, the phone still hadn't rung.

However, his mother, slender, brown-haired and attractive, caught his glance this time and seemed to recollect something with a start.

"My goodness!" Mrs. Andrews said. "I forgot. There was a message for you. Your friend Jupiter Jones called."

"He did?" Bob exclaimed. "What did he say?"

Bob had had the outlines of the case from Jupiter the day before. They had agreed that The Three Investigators would have a meeting that evening in Headquarters, if Jupe wasn't too busy. Sometimes he had to help his uncle and aunt at The Jones Salvage Yard and could not take any time off for investigating.

"I wrote it down." His mother began fishing around in her pocket among various scraps of paper. "I couldn't possibly remember it. Jupiter certainly does use strange language sometimes."

"He can't help talking in long words," Bob said. "He's read so much, the long words just come out automatically. Besides, his Uncle Titus talks that way, too. You get used to it."

"Well, anyway, here's the message." She found a piece of paper. " 'Red Gate Rover, come over, come over. The bird's on the wing and the case is the thing. The path will be narrow so follow the arrow.' Now honestly!"

She looked at Bob hard. "What kind of message is that, Robert? Are you boys playing at making up codes, or what?"

Bob was already halfway to the door, but he stopped, because when his mother asked a question she expected an answer.

"It's perfectly clear English, Mom," he said.

"Well, it doesn't sound like clear English to me," she retorted.

"It's clear English, but it *sounds* like a code," he explained. "That's so that if any outsider hears one of our messages, he won't understand it."

"And I'm an outsider, am I? Your own mother?"

"Well, gosh, no, Mom," Bob told her. "If you're interested I'll explain. You see, we've started this investigation firm, and right now we have a case. We're trying to find a missing parrot."

"Well, that sounds harmless enough," she said, her face clearing. "I suppose that's what 'The bird's on the wing, the case is the thing' means?"

"That's it. And Red Gate Rover means————"

"Oh, never mind. Run along now and don't be too late. I have to mail out invitations to the church supper we're having next week."

Bob hurried out and hopped on his bike. There was still plenty of daylight—it was summer, and they were on Daylight Saving. Rocky Beach was a spread-out town on the shore of the Pacific Ocean, some miles from Hollywood. It had a range of big hills behind it. Bob had fallen down one of these hills and banged up his leg so he now had to wear a brace on it. But it would come off some day, and on his bicycle he could make excellent time.

Sticking to the back streets, away from the heavy traffic by the beach, he reached The Jones Salvage Yard from the rear. It was probably the most colorful junk yard in the country. A long, tall wooden fence surrounded it, and on this fence local artists grateful to Mr. Jones for his generosity had painted many colorful scenes.

Covering the whole back fence of the yard was a painting of the San Francisco fire of 1906, a dramatic scene of burning buildings, horse-drawn fire engines dashing into action, and people fleeing with bundles on their backs.

Bob rode up to the rear fence, making sure no one saw him, and stopped about fifty feet from the corner. There was a spot on the picture where a big spout of red flame was shooting out of a building, and a little dog was sitting, looking sadly at it because it had been his home. They had named the little dog Rover, and one of his eyes was a knot in the wood.

Bob picked out the knot with his fingernails and reached in to undo a catch. Then three boards swung up and he could wheel his bike inside. That was Red Gate Rover.

There were four different secret gates into the junk yard so that The Three Investigators could, if necessary, come and go without being seen.

Once inside, he parked the bike and got down on his hands and knees. There were some building materials piled there, forming what looked like a cave. On top of the pile was an old sign with a large black arrow and the word *Office*. That was their secret joke. The arrow really did point to Headquarters.

Bob crawled under the pile of building material and came out in a narrow corridor with junk piled on both sides. This passage twisted and turned until he had to get down on his knees again and crawl under some heavy planks that seemed merely to be lying there, but were actually the roof of Door Four, one of the entrances into Headquarters.

He crawled a few feet, then was able to stand up. He knocked on a panel, three times, once, twice. The panel opened and Bob stooped to step into Headquarters.

Headquarters was inside a banged-up thirty-foot mobile home trailer in the junk yard, quite hidden from view by all kinds of junk stacked all around it. Even Mr. Jones didn't know that they had turned the old trailer into a modern headquarters, with a darkroom, a special lab, and an office with typewriter, telephone, desk and tape-recorder. All of the equipment had been rebuilt from junk that came into the yard. Except the telephone, naturally. They paid for that out of money they made helping around the junk yard.

Once the boys were inside, their conferences were completely secret.

Jupiter was sitting in a swivel chair, chewing on a pencil. Pete Crenshaw was doodling, drawing pictures of parrots over and over.

"Hello, Bob," Jupiter said. "What kept you?"

"Mom forgot your message," Bob told him. "Anyway, she wouldn't have let me leave without supper. Is this a super-secret meeting?"

Jupiter nodded. "Because of Aunt Mathilda," he said. "She's been cleaning house all day and she's had me helping her. Now she wants me to wash all the windows. Naturally, I shall do so, but it is imperative we make some progress in our search for Billy Shakespeare and Little Bo-Peep. I'm trying to think of some line of investigation for you two to start before I go to become a window washer."

The speech was typical of Jupiter Jones, who had been reading everything he could put his hands on for years. He couldn't seem to think in short words.

"We're stumped," Pete said. "Stuck. Baffled. We know that fat man who called himself Mr. Claudius must have stolen Billy Shakespeare and Little Bo-Peep, but we can't think of any way to locate him. The police might be able to find the car, but they wouldn't take the case seriously. Imagine if we went to Chief Reynolds here in town and asked for help in finding Shakespeare and Little Bo-Peep!"

"In any case, both Mr. Fentriss and Miss Waggoner swore us to secrecy," Jupiter said. "Yet somehow we must locate this Mr. Claudius or admit failure."

"Well, I have an idea," Bob said. "Let's just ask people if they've seen Mr. Claudius' car. If we ask enough people, someone is sure to have noticed it. And if we find the car, he's bound to be someplace near it."

"People," Jupiter said, "are very unobservant. Even eyewitnesses to an occurrence contradict each other."

"Not kids," Bob said. "Kids are very observant of anything that interests them. A lot of boys are interested in cars. If we asked a few thousand boys all around Los Angeles and Hollywood, I'll bet we'd turn up one who remembered the car perfectly."

Jupiter had that look on his face which meant his mental machinery was in overdrive. "Your idea is brilliant, Bob."

"It is?" Bob stared at him. "You really mean brilliant?"

"Ingeniously simple and therefore brilliant," Jupiter said. "As you state, boys of all ages are interested in cars, especially unusual cars. We must ask boys all over town

until we find one who has seen the car. Then we'll know
Mr. Claudius is near. But obviously we cannot ask each
boy personally."

"Then how'll we do it?" Pete asked blankly.

Jupiter leaned forward and looked at them.

"We'll use a Ghost-to-Ghost Hookup," he declared.

Chapter 5

A Ghost-to-Ghost Hookup

THEIR STOCKY PARTNER looked at them as if they knew what he was talking about. But Pete and Bob didn't have the foggiest idea what he meant.

"What's a Ghost-to-Ghost Hookup?" they asked at the same time.

"It is a method of contacting thousands of boys for information without speaking to them directly."

"Where do the ghosts come in?" Bob asked.

"There are no actual ghosts involved," Jupiter said. "However, the boys we contact won't know us, most of them, and we won't know them. To us they will be just voices on the telephone. If we call them 'ghosts,' it will be quite appropriate. Also, it will be a name that has flavor and color."

"It sure does have flavor and color," Bob agreed.

"In addition"—Jupiter was just getting well wound up —"when we refer to these unknown informants as 'ghosts,' no one who hears us will have any idea of what we are talking about. It will be our secret."

"Well, that makes sense," Pete agreed.

"And a last consideration," Jupiter told them. "My scheme could be used for contacting boys all the way from here to the Atlantic Ocean, if necessary. That would make it a Coast-to-Coast Hookup. But such a phrase has been used in the past by the radio and television networks. I prefer to be distinctive. So we will call ours a Ghost-to-Ghost Hookup."

"If you invented it, I guess you can call it anything you want," Pete said.

"Sure," Bob agreed. "But how does it work?"

"It works very simply. How many friends do you have living around here, Bob?"

"Oh, ten or twelve, I guess," Bob told him. "Why?"

"You'll see in a moment. Pete, how many friends do you have that are different from Bob's friends?"

"Six or seven," Pete said. "What are you getting at?"

"You will see in a moment. I have four or five friends who are different from the friends of you both. Now, Pete, will you describe Mr. Claudius' car again? And Bob, you write the description down."

"Two-door, sports model Ranger, color—black," Pete said. "Red leather upholstery. Practically new. It has a California license plate with a number ending in 13."

Bob wrote this down. Jupiter said, "And the driver, who calls himself Mr. Claudius, is quite fat and wears extremely strong glasses. I think that is enough description. Now we must start the hookup working.

"This is our method of procedure. First I will call five friends and ask them if they have seen the black Ranger. Assuming they haven't, I will ask them to call five friends, pass along the description, and ask those five each to call five more. They in turn will call five more, and so on until we get results. Each individual called will be given this telephone number. Anyone who can give us information about the car is to call us back here tomorrow morning at ten o'clock and relay the information to us.

"Now, is the procedure clear?"

"Hey, Jupe," Bob said, "that's terrific!"

"Wow!" Pete broke in. "By morning every boy in Southern California will be looking for that black Ranger."

"If necessary," Jupiter said. "Do either of you see any flaws in the scheme before we begin?"

"Shouldn't we offer a reward?" Pete asked. "It's customary to offer a reward for information."

"That's right," Bob said. "It'll keep everybody more interested."

"An excellent point." Jupiter was thinking hard. "But what can we offer? We haven't any money to speak of."

"How about offering a ride in the Rolls-Royce?" Pete suggested. "Any boy in town who likes cars would enjoy a ride in a gold-plated Rolls-Royce. And we could let him phone some of his friends from the car telephone to tell them about it."

"I believe you have a good point there," Jupiter agreed. "Bob, you had a suggestion?"

"I was going to say," Bob put in, "that we could let the first one to give us information have his choice of something from the junk yard. Why, the average kid could find a dozen things he wanted in this yard!"

"That's right," Pete agreed. "I don't know anybody who wouldn't enjoy having a chance to pick out something from all the wonderful kinds of junk your Uncle Titus brings back, Jupe."

"But we don't own the junk," Jupiter said, frowning. "We can't give away something that we don't own."

For a minute that had them all bothered. Then Pete remembered that Mr. Jones owed them something for work they had done helping repair items that he could resell. They added it up, and together the three of them had $25.13 coming. So they agreed that as a reward for information they would offer a ride in the gold-plated Rolls-Royce and anything in the junk yard valued at not more than $25.13.

With that settled, they started phoning. Jupiter phoned his five friends. None of them had seen the black car, but they all agreed to phone five more friends and pass the message along.

After Jupiter had called, he hurried out through Tunnel Two, their main entrance and exit, to wash windows for his Aunt Mathilda. Pete phoned next, and then Bob. It didn't take much explanation. Every boy they talked to caught on quickly, and was tickled to be in on an important investigation.

Even before they finished phoning, Bob and Pete knew the first ones they had talked to were spreading the message.

Bob stayed at Headquarters, typing up his notes about the case so far. When he got home an hour later, his mother was just hanging up the telephone with a puzzled look on her face.

"I can't understand it," she said. "I just can't understand it."

"What's wrong, Mom?" Bob asked.

"I've been trying to telephone the women who are going to help me at the church supper. I've called twelve so far and would you believe it, every single line is busy."

Bob gulped. He had an idea of the reason.

"Do they all have boys about my age?" he asked.

"Yes, so I wouldn't be surprised if three or four lines were busy. But goodness, twelve in a row. Well, I'll try Mrs. Garrett."

"I think you'll have better luck if you wait a little while," Bob said. "I mean, something might be out of order."

"I suppose so," she said, but she was still staring at the telephone as he went up to his room.

In his room, Bob sat down and did a little figuring. Three times five, which was the number of calls they personally had made, was fifteen. If each of the fifteen called five more friends, that made seventy-five. Five times seventy-five was three hundred and seventy-five, and five times that was one thousand, eight hundred and seventy-five, and five times that——

Bob stared at his calculations and whistled. No wonder the telephones were giving out a busy signal. Jupiter didn't know his own strength when it came to ideas. The Ghost-to-Ghost Hookup was pure dynamite!

However, it was a short message, so it wouldn't take long to get spread around. He knew everything would be normal soon, so he began to study the notes he had made on *The Mystery of the Stuttering Parrot,* as he called it.

Something bothered him. It was probably something very simple, but he couldn't place it. It wasn't the question of why the fat man wanted to steal parrots—they had all agreed that was a mystery that would have to wait for further facts. But there was the mystery of why anyone should teach a parrot to stutter. Because obviously, as Jupiter had pointed out, Billy Shakespeare had been *taught* to say "To-to-to be or not to-to-to be," since a parrot couldn't possibly stutter by accident. And then——

But at that point, having got into bed, he drifted off to sleep. Sometime in the middle of the night, though, he woke up and in the silence almost seemed to hear a voice chanting in his ear, "Little Bo-Peep has lost her sheep and doesn't know where to find it. Call on Sherlock Holmes." That was what Bo-Peep said, as reported by Miss Waggoner.

However—forgetting the mysterious suggestion to call on Sherlock Holmes—the line was wrong. The real *Mother Goose* line, as Bob remembered it, went, "Little Bo-Peep has lost her sheep and doesn't know where to find them."

But the parrot named Bo-Peep didn't say *them,* it said *it.*

Somehow, Bob had a feeling Jupe was going to find that important.

"Mmm." Jupiter twisted his round face into a mask of thoughtful concentration. "You're right, Bob. Miss Waggoner definitely reported that her parrot said, '. . . doesn't know where to find *it*.' Now of course, the word sheep is both singular and plural, so either *it* or *them* is correct. However——"

"Never mind all the educated talk!" Pete groaned. "What does it mean?"

The three boys were gathered in Headquarters, the following morning. It was a few minutes before ten o'clock, at which time they hoped for some results from the Ghost-to-Ghost Hookup they had put into effect the night before. Meanwhile, they were discussing Bob's discovery.

"Of course," Bob put in now, "it could just be a mistake. The Englishman who taught the parrots didn't remember the line correctly."

"Correction," Jupiter said. "Billy Shakespeare stuttered. That could be called a mistake. Little Bo-Peep speaks her line from *Mother Goose* incorrectly. That makes two mistakes."

"How many is two?" Pete asked impatiently. "I make a lot more than two mistakes every time I turn in a theme at school."

"Quite true," Jupiter agreed. "But in this case we feel sure the two parrots were taught by a well-educated Englishman. One mistake could be an accident. Two mistakes suggest purpose."

"Purpose?" Pete's face looked blank, and Bob didn't

blame him. It wasn't always easy to follow Jupiter's thinking. Sometimes his brain seemed to take short cuts.

"You mean it's just as easy to teach a parrot to say something correctly as it is to teach him to say something incorrectly?" Bob suggested. "So there's some special reason why Billy Shakespeare stutters and Little Bo-Peep says *it,* not *them?*"

"Exactly," Jupiter said. "First we have the peculiar mystery of why Mr. Claudius should go around stealing parrots. Then we have the new mystery of why the parrots were taught their strange speeches incorrectly to begin with."

"It beats me." Bob shook his head. "Why teach these parrots things like that anyway? Most people are satisfied if a parrot just says, 'Polly wants a cracker.'"

"The mystery deepens as we explore it," Jupiter said. His face had that look of real satisfaction which only came when he knew he had a good, tough puzzle—something he could sink his teeth into.

"Teaching the parrots took a great deal of patience," he went on. "Whoever did it had some purpose in mind. We don't know what that purpose was. However, I suspect that Mr. Claudius does know, and that's the reason he stole the two parrots."

"Wow!" Bob said. "Maybe there are a lot more parrots in this than just Billy and Bo-Peep. Remember the one named Blackbeard the peddler hadn't sold, and how excited Mr. Claudius became when he heard about it?"

"Oh, no!" Pete groaned. "If two parrots can make us

feel so bird-brained, think what a lot more would do to us!"

Ordinarily they would have laughed. But just at that moment the phone rang. Jupiter grabbed it as if it might have been planning to fly away.

"Hello, Jupiter Jones speaking," he said. "Yes, that's right. I'm the one seeking information about . . . You did? First tell me, did it have a license plate that ended in thirteen? . . . Oh, it didn't? . . . I'm very sorry, but it wasn't the car we are trying to trace. Thank you just the same, though."

He hung up, looking disappointed.

"A boy in Hollywood," he said. "But it was the wrong license plate."

The phone rang again. This time he remembered to hold it near the loudspeaker he'd made so the others could hear the conversation. It was a boy in Santa Monica, who had seen a black Ranger parked outside a restaurant the night before. But a young couple had driven off in it, and it was several years old. Wrong car again.

In all, there were eight more calls. Jupiter expertly questioned everyone who called, but it was obviously the wrong car every time.

The Ghost-to-Ghost Hookup had been a dud! They still didn't have a clue to lead them to Mr. Claudius.

Chapter 6

An Unexpected Visitor

THE BOYS WERE looking at each other, very disappointed, when Jupiter's aunt, Mathilda Jones, began calling him. Mathilda Jones was a large woman, with a very powerful voice, and they could hear her without difficulty.

"Jupiter!" Mrs. Jones was calling. "Somebody here to see you! Jupiter, where are you? Sakes and goodness, where did you go? I saw you around here only an hour ago. There's a boy here who wants to see you. A Mexican boy."

A Mexican boy! They all had the same thought. The man who sold the parrots had spoken with a Mexican accent!

They made a dash for Tunnel Two. There was a square section of the floor that opened, and underneath it was a large corrugated pipe. They dropped into the pipe and crawled along about forty feet. Then they came to a movable chunk of iron grating. Pete, who was in front, pushed this aside, and they crawled out of Tunnel Two behind the rebuilt printing press, where they printed their business cards and letterheads.

They were in Jupiter's outdoor workshop. It was in a corner of the junk yard where nobody could see them because of the way things were piled up. Jupiter had his power saw and drill press and other things he had rebuilt from the junk his Uncle Titus bought, under the six-foot roof that ran around the inside of the fence that closed in the junk yard.

Southern California is rather dry. They could work outdoors most of the time, and had plastic covers to protect everything whenever the weather happened to turn bad.

Mrs. Jones was still calling. They all ducked around a couple of piles of junk and came out into the main part of the yard, near the front gate and the office.

"You called me, Aunt Mathilda?" Jupiter asked, and his aunt turned around. Behind her they saw a Mexican boy, about as tall as Bob, wearing very ragged pants and a torn shirt. He was holding the reins of a small donkey that was pulling an old, two-wheeled donkey cart.

"This boy wants to see you, Jupiter," Mrs. Jones said. "You can take it easy today, I'm sure you'll be delighted to know. But tomorrow there will be lots of work to be done. Titus is coming back from a buying trip."

"Yes, Aunt Mathilda," Jupiter said.

Mrs. Jones went back into the office of The Jones Salvage Yard. The Mexican boy was looking all around, his black eyes shifting this way and that. Then he turned to Jupiter, which was natural because Jupiter's shape, stocky but compact, attracted the eye.

"Señor Jupiter?" he asked.

"I'm Jupiter Jones," Jupiter said.

"I am Carlos," the boy said. He had a liquid Mexican accent, which sounded almost musical. "The au-to, it is where? May I see it?"

"The au-to?" Jupiter didn't get it, but Pete did.

"He wants to know where the Rolls-Royce is," he said.

"Oh. The car is in the garage," Jupiter told Carlos.

"A golden au-to!" Carlos said. "It must be beautiful. I wish so much to see it." He started to grin at them, then looked frightened. "Excuse me, Señor Jupiter, but the cars, I like them so much. All cars. Someday . . . someday I too shall own a car!"

"You've come here about cars?" Jupiter asked. He looked around. Hans and Konrad, his uncle's two husky, blond Bavarian helpers, were just driving the smaller truck in the gate. "Come this way."

Carlos hesitated a second, then he tied the reins of his donkey to a piece of pipe and followed Jupiter. Before he left it he patted the little gray donkey affectionately.

"Soon I return, Pablo," he told the donkey.

In a minute they were all sitting down in the outdoor workshop area. Carlos looked around wide-eyed at all the apparatus.

"Carlos, did you come to tell us about a black sports model Ranger?" Jupiter asked.

Carlos nodded his head so hard it looked as if it might snap off.

"*Sí, sí, sí*, Señor Jupiter," he said. "Last night my friend Esteban come to my house. He say a Señor Jupiter Jones wish to know about a Ranger car with a license number that ends in one—three."

The boys waited, holding their breath. Carlos looked at them with eyes that were wide with hope.

"And"—he paused—"he said there was a re-ward."

"A reward!" Pete howled, so excitedly that Carlos looked frightened. "You bet there is! Did you see the car? Do you know where it is?"

"Oh yes, I see the car," Carlos said. "I see the fat man. But where now he is I do not know. It was"—he counted on his fingers—"one—two—seven—seven days ago I see the car and the fat man."

"Seven days!" Pete said, disappointed. "That isn't much help. How can you remember a car after a week?"

"Oh, I like the cars so much," Carlos said. "I dream about the cars. The black Ranger, he is a beautiful car. I can tell you license number. AK four—five—one—three. Seats, all covered with red leather. Small scratch on right front fender. Little dent in rear bumper."

They all looked at him with a new respect. Many boys can identify the make and year of almost any car they see, but not many could remember such details as a license number, and a scratch, a full week later.

"That would help the police locate him," Jupiter said, pinching his lip. "But we are pledged at this point not to go to the police. You haven't seen the car lately, have you, Carlos?"

The Mexican boy shook his head, his brown eyes sad.

"Can not win re-ward?" he asked. "Can not"—he

heaved a sigh—"ride in so wonderful golden au-to?"

"Perhaps, Carlos," Jupiter said. "First of all, how did you happen to see the car and Mr. Claudius—that's the fat man?"

"He came to see my Uncle Ramos," Carlos said, "for the parrots."

"The parrots?" Pete shouted. "Then it was your uncle who sold Billy Shakespeare and Little Bo-Peep?"

Carlos nodded. "And the others, too," he said. "All the parrots with the strange names."

"Strange names?" Jupiter asked, as he and Bob exchanged quick glances. So Bob's hunch about there being more parrots involved in the case was right! "Can you remember the names?"

Carlos ran his hand through his thick black hair. Then he nodded.

"I remember them," he said. "There was Billy Shakespeare and Little Bo-Peep."

The other boys nodded. "We know about them," Pete said.

"Then there was Sher-lock Holmes and Robin Hood," Carlos continued.

"Sherlock Holmes and Robin Hood," Bob repeated, writing the names down.

"Captain Kidd and Scarface," Carlos added. "Scarface, he has only one eye."

Bob wrote down the two additional names.

"That makes six," he said. "Were there any more?"

"Oh, yes." Carlos' face lighted up. "The dark one. Blackbeard the Pirate, the one who talk so good. Seven parrots, all with pretty yellow heads. Except Blackbeard. He did not have a yellow head."

"Blackbeard the Pirate!" Bob exclaimed, writing the name down. "That's the one Mr. Fentriss mentioned and that Mr. Claudius got excited about. Hey, Jupe, do you suppose all seven are involved in this case?"

"We'll find out," Jupiter replied. "Carlos, you say the fat man came to see your Uncle Ramos a week ago to get these parrots?"

"*Sí*, he came for them."

"And did your uncle let him have them?"

"No, señor." A look of sadness crossed Carlos' face. "Uncle Ramos—he had already sold all the parrots. The fat man—he would pay one thousand dollars for them. But Uncle Ramos did not have them any more. And the fat man got very excited, and he say nasty things about Uncle Ramos when Uncle Ramos say he cannot remember who he sell them to. Because you see, Señor Jupiter, my uncle cannot read or write. So he just sell the parrots and take the money."

"So Mr. Claudius has been trying to locate the parrots ever since, and for some unknown reason, stealing those he could find!" Jupiter exclaimed to Bob and Pete. "We are gaining a great deal of information. The Ghost-to-Ghost Hookup has produced results after all, even if it did not turn up the exact whereabouts of Mr. Claudius."

"If you ask me, we're getting too much information," Pete said. "We started out with one missing parrot to find. Then we had two. Now I bet you're thinking of trying to find all seven, aren't you?"

Jupiter did not deny the fact.

"All seven birds are part of the same mystery," he said. "To solve the mystery, we should find the birds."

"But we only promised to try to get back Billy Shakespeare and Little Bo-Peep," Pete said. "We didn't bargain on solving some weird mystery too."

Bob knew Pete was wasting his breath. Pete knew it, too. Giving Jupiter Jones a mystery to solve was like giving a juicy bone to a bulldog. He wouldn't let it go until he was through with it.

Jupiter turned to the Mexican boy. "Carlos," he said, "we appreciate the information you've given us, but why didn't you telephone? Why did you drive all the way to Rocky Beach in your donkey cart to see us?"

"I had the hope," Carlos told him, "to take home the re-ward in the donkey cart. And besides, Señor Jupiter, I did not have any money for a telephone call."

The three boys looked at each other. The same thought was in all their minds. Sometimes they were strapped for money, but they always had an allowance coming in, or could do something around the junk yard to earn a little. It was hard to realize that some people didn't have any money—not any at all.

Bob saw Jupiter swallow a couple of times as he took another look at Carlos and saw how skinny he was.

"I see," he said. "Well, you've given us some very valuable information and that's worth a part reward anyway. You see, what we were really hoping to do was locate the car and that way get an idea where Mr. Claudius lives."

"Where the fat man live?" Carlos brightened. "Oh, now I understand."

He fished into his pocket for something.

"When the fat man leave my Uncle Ramos," he said, "he promise him much money if he remember where he sell all the parrots. He give him this card."

He handed Jupiter a calling card. It had Mr. Claudius' name and address on it. The Ghost-to-Ghost Hookup had tracked down the fat man after all!

All three were trying to crowd around to see what the card said, as a red light over the printing press began to blink. Jupiter had installed it so that any time their private telephone in Headquarters rang they would know and could answer it secretly.

Somebody was phoning them now. Jupiter made a quick decision.

"Carlos," he said, "close your eyes."

"*Sí*, Señor Jupiter," Carlos said and closed his eyes.

"Pete, stay with Carlos. Bob and I have business to attend to. We'll be right back."

While Carlos had his eyes closed, Bob and Jupiter ducked back into the big corrugated pipe that was Tunnel Two, crawled through and into Headquarters. Jupe grabbed up the phone.

"Hello," said a voice. It was a woman's voice, and she was speaking very softly, as if afraid of being overheard. "Are you the boy named Jupiter Jones who is trying to locate Mr. Claudius' car?"

"Yes, ma'am," Jupiter said. "Can you tell me where it is?"

"It's been garaged where no one can see it!" The woman sounded almost angry. "And you mustn't try to find Mr. Claudius, do you hear? He has a very violent temper and it's dangerous to cross him. Whatever you do, stay away from him. Don't interfere in his affairs!"

She hung up. Jupiter and Bob sat staring at each other. In his hand Jupiter still held the card that told them exactly where to find Mr. Claudius. Except that after the unknown woman's warning——

Slowly Jupiter put the card into his pocket.

"We must pay Carlos his reward," he said to Bob after a moment of silence. "Then we must go to his home to see what his uncle can tell us. I'm sure we are on the verge of learning a great deal. After that—well, after that there will be time enough to think about dealing with Mr. Claudius."

It was an odd procession that started south along the coast road a couple of hours later. Leading the procession was the huge old Rolls-Royce with gold-plated fittings. Worthington, of course, was driving, and Jupiter, Pete and Carlos were in the rear seat. Bob had had to go to the library to work.

Carlos could hardly keep his excitement in check. He ran his fingers over the gold plating, touched the tanned leather covering the seats, and stared wide-eyed at the gold-plated telephone, with which the car was equipped.

"A golden au-to!" he kept repeating. "Such beauty! Never did I have the dream of riding in such an au-to."

Carlos knew cars, that was apparent. Every car that passed he could identify by make, year and model, no matter how swiftly it whizzed by. His ambition was to be an auto mechanic, he told them, and have a garage of his own.

Behind the Rolls-Royce came the junk yard's smaller truck, with Konrad driving it. In the truck was the reward which the three boys agreed Carlos had fully earned. What he had asked for from the junk yard was a little surprising, though. He had wanted scrap lumber and a door and a window and some nails—to fix up the house where he and his uncle lived, he confided. It needed many repairs.

Jupiter had whispered to his aunt that Carlos and his uncle had no money. Mrs. Jones, whose heart was as big as she was, had put a very low price on all the material. It had not only come within the $25.13 figure which she owed The Three Investigators, but Mrs. Jones calculated the bill so generously that there was ten dollars left over, which she gave to Carlos in cash.

All the lumber, the window and door and nails and a can of paint thrown in, however, were far too much to load on the donkey cart drawn by little gray Pablo. The problem of how to get Pablo and the cart back home was solved by Hans and Konrad. They just lifted Pablo and the cart into the truck, along with the building materials. Now Pablo was having his own ride in the truck behind the Rolls-Royce, peering curiously over the sides at everything he passed.

Eventually the procession of car and truck entered a section of very small and very run-down houses, with open fields where some crops were being grown. This was the neighborhood where Carlos lived. Boys and girls came running out to stare at the Rolls-Royce. Carlos waved to them.

"José!" he shouted. "Esteban! Margarita! See! I ride in the golden au-to!"

Presently there were so many ragged children crowding around that Worthington had to stop the car. They all wanted to touch the Rolls Royce, but Carlos spoke to them sharply in Spanish, and they drew back.

"Shall I proceed now, Master Jones?" Worthington asked. He never lost his temper, no matter what happened.

"No, Worthington," the boy told him. "The truck hasn't caught up with us yet. We don't want to lose it."

As they waited, Carlos pointed across a vacant lot. A block farther on was a tumble-down shanty with an old greenhouse behind it.

"There I live," he said. "Uncle Ramos and I. We can walk there. We do not need to ride in this beautiful au-to all the way. The road is very bad."

Jupiter accepted the suggestion, and all three boys clambered out.

"Thank you, Worthington," Jupiter said. "We will not need to drive back with you. We can ride back in the truck with Konrad."

"Very good, Master Jones," Worthington said, and the big car drove off. Then the truck drove up and Jupiter pointed out the shack to Konrad.

"Meet us there, Konrad," he called, and the husky Bavarian nodded. Jupiter and Pete and Carlos started across the open field toward the house—if you could call it a house—where Carlos lived. The closer they got to it, the more dilapidated it looked. One wall was almost gone, a window was out and the door was missing.

Carlos seemed to sense their thoughts.

"When my uncle come from Mexico, he have no money," he said. "This place is only place he can stay. Rent is twenty dollars a month." He patted his pocket where the ten-dollar bill that Mrs. Jones had given him reposed. "Now I pay rent for two more weeks," he said happily. "I fix house well, then Uncle Ramos' cough get better and he can work again."

As they were talking, they approached the rear of the house. In the dirt road beyond the house they could see a car parked. It was an ordinary black sedan of popular make, but Carlos scowled.

"Who calls on Uncle Ramos?" he asked. "I do not like this."

He began to hurry, and Pete and Jupiter ran after him. As they came closer to the tumble-down shack they could hear a voice raised inside—a loud, angry voice.

"That's Mr. Claudius' voice," Pete said to his stocky partner.

"Tell me!" Mr. Claudius was shouting. "Tell me, you old idiot, or I'll wring your neck!"

"Uncle Ramos!" Carlos cried, breaking into a run. "What does the fat one do to you?"

Now he was ahead of them, and Pete and Jupiter ran to keep up. As Carlos burst into the house through the doorless entrance, they were at his heels. They were in time to see Mr. Claudius, his back to them, bent over a bed on which a man, undoubtedly Carlos' uncle, lay. The uncle was coughing and choking, and it looked as if the fat man was trying to throttle him.

"You *have* to remember!" Mr. Claudius was shouting. "Even if you can't remember where you sold the other parrots, you have to remember about Blackbeard. You still had him after you sold the rest. I have four of them now, and I'll get the rest, but I must have Blackbeard. I'm sure you know where he is!"

Carlos, bursting into the room, flung himself like a small terrier straight at the fat man's legs. Mr. Claudius heard him, however, and whirled. With one hand he seemed to grab the small Mexican boy out of mid-air. Suddenly Carlos was dangling helplessly, his feet off the ground, Mr. Claudius' hand clenching the collar of his ragged shirt.

"Stand back," Mr. Claudius said, in a quiet but ugly voice, as Pete and Jupiter hesitated, "or I'll wring this little rooster's neck. And then yours."

"Grab him!" Carlos cried, almost in tears, not from fright but from anger. "He hurt my uncle, who is sick and cannot defend himself."

"Stand quietly," Mr. Claudius warned, his eyes glinting dangerously. "You boys are becoming quite a nuisance to me."

At that moment, Carlos' ragged shirt ripped. The Mexican boy fell to the floor and immediately flung his arms around the fat man's legs. Pete and Jupiter leaped to his aid. Pete gave a flying tackle to get his arms around

Mr. Claudius' waist, and Jupiter chose to try to aid Carlos in holding his legs.

But deceptive muscles lurked beneath Mr. Claudius' pudginess. He flung Carlos aside and turned so that Pete and Jupiter seemed to bounce off him and go sailing to separate sides of the room. Then he was at the door, running out, before they could pick themselves up.

By the time they got to their feet, they saw him leap into the sedan and roar off, just as Konrad, unaware of what had happened, parked the salvage-yard truck immediately behind him.

"If only we could have held him until Konrad got here," Pete said gloomily, brushing himself off.

"Or if I hadn't dismissed Worthington, we could pursue him," Jupiter added, as they watched the sedan disappear around a corner. "However, we do have his name and address."

"That's good," Pete said. "That tells us what part of town to stay away from. That Mr. Claudius doesn't like The Three Investigators."

"He is angry, and anger arises from fear," Jupiter told him. "He is now afraid of us. That gives us a definite advantage."

"He's afraid of *us!*" Pete exclaimed. "How do you think we feel about *him?*"

"Nervous but confident."

"That sentence is two words too long."

They turned from the door. Carlos was giving his uncle a drink of water to ease a spasm of coughing.

Pete picked up a chair that had been knocked over—

the only chair in the room—and they approached the bed. Carlos turned.

"I thank you one thousand times," he said, "for aiding me to chase away that fat one. He came to try to make Uncle Ramos tell him to whom he sold the parrot named Blackbeard. Uncle Ramos could not tell him because he does not remember. It was some lady who live two block, three block, maybe four block away, but he does not know her name. She buy him for only ten dollars as no one else wanted him. The fat one was very anxious to find him."

"He certainly was anxious," Pete said. "Mr. Claudius knows something about those birds that we don't know."

"Something that makes them very important to him," Jupiter said. "I wonder what——"

They were interrupted by a knock on the door. It was Konrad.

"You want I unload the materials now?" he asked.

"Yes, pile them beside the house," Jupiter said. Then he and Pete caught sight of an elderly woman behind Konrad, carrying a cardboard box with holes punched in it. "Who is that?" Jupiter asked.

"A lady who was walking this way. I give her a lift," Konrad said. "Hokay, I unload."

He turned aside and the elderly woman who had been behind him marched up to the door. She looked suspiciously at Pete and Jupiter.

"Who are you boys?" she asked. "Where is that rascal Ramos?"

Carlos pushed between the two partners.

"My uncle is sick," he said. "I am Carlos. What do you want?"

"My money back!" the woman said emphatically. "Your uncle sold me this bird saying he was a rare parrot, and my son-in-law says I've been swindled because he isn't. He's just some kind of starling. And besides, what he says is not fit for decent ears."

She thrust the box into Carlos' arms.

"Now give me my ten dollars!" she said. "I won't be swindled. Imagine telling me a starling is a parrot!"

Carlos looked unhappy. He handed the box to Pete, and slowly put his hand into his pocket. He brought out the tightly folded ten-dollar bill which he had received from Mrs. Jones. Pete and Jupiter knew how much it meant to him. It was the only money he had. Yet he managed to smile as he handed it to the woman.

"Pardon, señora," he said. "My uncle is ill. He make a mistake. Your money, here it is."

"Humph, a starling!" the woman said and stalked off.

Carlos turned toward Jupiter and Pete.

"It must be Blackbeard," he said. "He talk so well, my uncle and I, we are sure he is some kind of rare parrot."

He opened the box, and a small dark bird with a large yellow bill shook itself, fluffed its feathers, and suddenly flapped its wings. It sailed upward and alighted on Pete's shoulder.

"Why, that's no starling!" Jupiter exclaimed excitedly. "That's a mynah bird. They can be taught to talk even better than parrots. Well-trained ones are quite valuable."

"I'm Blackbeard the Pirate!" the mynah bird suddenly

exclaimed, in a raucous, piratical voice. "I've buried my treasure where dead men guard it ever! Yo-ho-ho and a bottle of rum!"

Then it burst into a string of expressions the boys knew their families would never approve of. But they scarcely heard the words in their excitement.

"Blackbeard!" Jupiter exclaimed. "The bird Mr. Claudius wants so badly. And we have him!"

At that moment, Blackbeard, looking around hungrily, saw Pete's ear temptingly close. He nipped it. Pete gave a yell and batted Blackbeard into the air. The bird flapped its wings, then soared off skyward.

"It's gone!" Jupiter said. "Pete, you've just lost us a very valuable clue!"

"And it's lost me some very valuable blood," Pete muttered, applying his handkerchief to his ear as they watched Blackbeard disappear behind a clump of trees. Despite his words, Pete felt pretty low. The mynah bird's remark about buried treasure and dead men guarding it had sounded even more mysterious than the queer things reported said by Billy Shakespeare and Bo-Peep. He felt sure that his stocky partner was right, that a very important clue had been in their hands—or at least, on his shoulder.

And he had chased it away!

Chapter 7

Mysterious Treasure

BY THE TIME it was apparent that Blackbeard, the talking mynah bird, was not coming back, Carlos had soothed his uncle so that the man could speak without coughing. He lay back in bed and tried to answer the questions that Jupiter asked. But it was easier for him to answer in Spanish, so that finally Carlos took up the story for him, while his uncle lay and rested, sometimes nodding his head and saying, *"Sí, sí!"*

"Two years ago, my Uncle Ramos come here," Carlos told Pete and Jupiter. "He drive up from Mexico in donkey cart pulled by Pablo. My uncle is very good with growing flowers. But he cannot get job here. Someone tell him about this place, with old greenhouse, much glass broken. He rent it for twenty dollar a month and raise flowers."

The two boys nodded. Judging by the condition of the shack, wide open to the outdoors, twenty dollars a month was plenty to pay for it.

"Uncle Ramos, he fix greenhouse with old tin cans pounded out flat. Some flowers he grow outdoors. Special rare flowers he grow in greenhouse. He take flowers in donkey cart to sell in city.

"One day tall, thin man come down the road to our house. This man is name John Silver, and he say he come from England. He is weak and sick and have not much money. He ask Uncle Ramos to let him stay, and my uncle say all right.

"Señor Silver have only some clothes in a sailor's bag, and a box, a metal box. It is long and flat and wide, so, like this."

Carlos held his hands apart in two different positions and his uncle said, "Sí! Sí!" nodding vigorously. Jupiter made a quick calculation.

"About fourteen inches by twenty-four," he said. "Go on, Carlos. You're giving us a lot of information."

"This box, it has strong lock on it," the other boy said. "Mr. Silver sleep with it under mattress. Every night he open it and look inside, and when he look inside, his face, it seems happy."

Again his uncle nodded and cried, "*Sí! Sí!* Ver' happy!"

"Uncle Ramos ask Mr. Silver what is in box. Mr. Silver laugh and say——" Carlos scratched his thick thatch of unruly black hair, trying to remember the words—— "he say, 'This box hold piece off the end of the rainbow, with pot of gold underneath it.' "

"A piece off the end of the rainbow, with a pot of gold underneath it," Jupiter repeated, his round features scowling. "A most mystifying description. Go on, Carlos," Jupiter urged.

"Well, Señor Jupiter," the Mexican boy said, "Uncle

Ramos catch cough. He is not well, so he send for me. I hitchhike to get here and try to help, but I do not have the experience with flowers. I am no good to him."

"You are good boy!" his uncle said, in English. "Fine boy! Work hard!"

"Thank you, Uncle Ramos." Carlos brightened. "Anyway, Mr. Silver is also sick. He say sickness inside of him, will not go away. I ask him why he does not take pot of gold from under rainbow he says he has in box, and go to good doctor. He laugh, and then look sad. He tell me he do not dare.

"He say——" Carlos drew a long breath, thinking hard to remember back——"he say if he try to sell pot of gold in box, he have to tell his real name and how he get it. But he is here in this country not legal, and he would be deported back to England where they want to put him in jail.

"So he has to live here, with no money, enjoying his piece of the rainbow as long as he can. Then he say it is all right, he will be going away soon anyway."

Carlos' young features clouded.

"I do not understand what he mean," he said. "Not until later. But one day Mr. Silver bring back to house seven young parrots, all with pretty yellow heads, and seven cages. He put them into the greenhouse and start to teach them to speak."

Pete and Jupiter looked at each other with quickened interest. At last they were about to learn something of the mystery behind the parrots.

"Mr. Silver very good with birds," Carlos said. "He

have Blackbeard, the bird that talks, with him when he comes. It ride on his shoulder all the time, and say swear words. This make Mr. Silver laugh.

"Now in greenhouse he start teaching parrots words. Each one different words. And he give them funny names. I do not understand names or words."

"The names mostly come from English literature or history," Jupiter said. "That's why you didn't recognize them. Do you remember any of the speeches he taught the parrots?"

"No." Carlos heaved a sigh. "Too hard for me to remember. But one parrot with yellow head die. Mr. Silver is much upset. Then he say Blackbeard will have to double for parrot. I do not know what that means."

"Here in Hollywood," Pete put in, "everybody knows what a double is. It's someone who takes the star's place for a stunt."

"Well, anyway, he finish teaching six yellow parrots and dark one, which he says is rare kind of parrot."

"He probably said that thinking if he called it a mynah bird it would confuse you," Jupiter suggested. "What happened when he had finished, Carlos?"

Carlos spread his hands in bewilderment.

"Mr. John Silver go away," he said. "In the night, he go away. He take metal box with him. He is gone three days. When he come back he is very weak, very sick, and has no metal box. He say he has hidden it. He say he must go soon, and he does not give us metal box with piece of rainbow in it because it would make us much trouble.

"Instead, he write long letter. He give it to me to mail."

"Do you remember to whom he mailed it?" Jupiter asked eagerly. But Carlos shook his head.

"No, Señor Jupiter. But it has many stamps on it and little red and blue stripes all around edge."

"An air mail letter," Pete suggested.

"Possibly to Europe, if it had a lot of stamps," Jupiter added.

"He say that soon he go away. He mean that he will die. He will not let us take him to hospital because he say no hospital can cure him. He say he want to be with friends." Carlos' voice was quiet at the memory.

"He is a very strange man, Mr. Silver. He make strange jokes, he talk in riddles, he teach parrots funny talk. But he is our friend. We know he is good!" Carlos was silent for a moment, then went on.

"Mr. Silver say that soon a very fat man come. He will give us one thousand dollars and we will give him the seven talking birds. He laugh very hard when he say this. He say that it is his best joke, that in all his life he has never made up a better joke than this. He say it is a joke that will make the fat man sweat very hard. He go to sleep laughing at his joke. Then in the morning—in the morning he does not wake up."

The Mexican boy swallowed hard. Both Pete and Jupiter could sense the sadness he felt.

"But the fat man didn't come, did he?" Jupiter asked at last. Carlos shook his head.

"Because Mr. Silver is our friend, we arrange that he

be bury in little churchyard down the street. We have no money, but we promise to pay soon. We wait one week, two week, three week. But fat man does not come. At last we think he will never come and Uncle Ramos hitch up Pablo and put parrots on cart and go from door to door to sell the parrots for money we need.

"The people like the parrots, even Scarface and Blackbeard, so he sell them all in one day and we have money. Only a little, but enough to pay for Mr. Silver's grave. Not enough to fix up house, though."

At last Carlos smiled.

"But now I have lumber, nails, door," he said. "I fix house. Soon Uncle Ramos is well again, and we are fine. Oh, I thank you one thousand times, Señor Jupiter."

"No, you've earned the reward and a lot more if we had it," Jupiter said earnestly. "But there's one more thing. The fat man finally did come, didn't he?"

"Oh yes." Carlos nodded and the sick man on the bed raised his head to chime in with, *"Sí! Sí!"*

"Two week after we sell the parrots, he come. He is very angry. He insult Uncle Ramos because he cannot read and write and does not know who he sell parrots to. Uncle Ramos tell him to leave and not come back. Then he beg and beg. I get map from gas station, Uncle Ramos show him part of town where he sell the parrots, and then the fat man go off in his Ranger sport car.

"But he leave his card, with his name and address and telephone number. He tell Uncle Ramos to let him know if he can remember anything more. But uncle cannot. It is too bad. One thousand dollars would be most nice to have. But we can live without it."

Carlos drew himself up proudly.

"We take care of our friend. We pay our debts. Some place I will find money for rent. Señor Fat Man cannot insult my uncle again."

Jupiter was thinking. Now they knew a lot more about the parrots than they had known before. But there was still a lot they didn't know. He was about to ask another question when Konrad, the big Bavarian helper, stepped through the doorless doorway. The boys had been so intent on the story they were hearing, they had forgotten he had been unloading the building materials from the truck.

"Everything unloaded," he said. "Ready we start back? Got lots of work to do at yard."

"I guess so," Jupiter said. "No, wait. Do you have a map of Los Angeles in the truck, Konrad?"

"Sure, got two, three," Konrad said. "You want one?"

"Pete will get it," Jupiter said.

Pete dashed out, found the maps, selected the one that showed the most streets, and brought it in.

"Carlos," Jupiter asked, "can you show us the part of town where your uncle sold the parrots?"

The boy shot a string of rapid words in Spanish to his uncle, who nodded. Sitting on the side of the bed, Carlos then drew lines with a pencil around a section on the map his uncle pointed out.

"Here, Señor Jupiter," he said. "Some place inside

these lines. But what streets, I am sorry my uncle cannot say."

Jupiter took the map, folded it, and put it in his pocket.

"Thanks, Carlos," he said. "We already have a general idea because we know who bought Billy Shakespeare and Little Bo-Peep. I guess we've learned everything we can for now, though at the moment the mystery seems more mystifying than ever."

"I'll buy that," Pete said.

"If only we hadn't lost Blackbeard——" Jupiter began. "But a good investigator must always expect setbacks."

He shook hands with Carlos.

"I hope your uncle gets better soon," he said. "If Mr. Claudius comes around again bothering your uncle, get the police. They'll take care of him."

"The police, ha!" The other boy's dark eyes flashed. He picked up a cane standing against the table. "Señor Fat Man will need the hospital!"

Admiringly, Pete and Jupiter felt pretty sure he would, too.

They left him standing there with the cane in his hand, and went out and climbed in the truck. All the way back to Rocky Beach Jupiter sat with his head hunched, pinching his lower lip, his mental gears spinning so hard Pete could almost hear them whir.

When they got back to The Jones Salvage Yard, Pete ventured to ask Jupiter what he had figured out.

"I want to sleep on it before I try to figure out the

meaning of what we know so far," his partner told him. "We must begin tomorrow by rechecking our facts. Frankly, this case has taken on aspects which puzzle me."

"They don't puzzle me a bit," Pete told him. "They just baffle me completely. Jupe, couldn't you talk plain English once in a while? I mean, just for a change. Couldn't you say this case is a real skull-buster?"

Jupiter looked at him intently.

"All right," he agreed. "I'll say it. This case is a real skull-buster!"

Chapter 8

Blackbeard the Pirate

THE NEXT MORNING, Bob Andrews rode his bike through the main gate of The Jones Salvage Yard and saw right away that The Three Investigators weren't likely to have a conference that morning. Pete and Jupiter were hard at work, while Mrs. Mathilda Jones supervised.

The minute he got inside, Mrs. Jones spotted him.

"You're just in time, Bob Andrews!" she called. "We're taking inventory today."

Mrs. Jones had a very big heart but when she saw a boy, she had only one idea—to put him to work! She had Pete and Jupiter working so hard they scarcely had time to mop the sweat off their faces. They were counting bathtubs and sinks, lifting bunches of iron rods to count them, moving other junk to see what was behind it, and calling out the amount to Mrs. Jones.

"One 18-foot I-beam!" Pete called.

"One 18-foot I-beam," Mrs. Jones said, and wrote it down. Then, as Bob got there, she handed the pad and pencil to him. "You take over, Bob."

He barely had time to grab the pencil before Jupiter yelled, "Twelve cast-iron sinks!" Bob wrote it down. Then Jupiter moved over close and whispered, "We're trying to make some money, Bob. I have an idea I want to try out."

They were working busily when Bob noticed that Mrs. Jones was poking around near their Headquarters. She was looking at the big stack of old rusty boilers, steel pipes, building material and other large pieces of junk that Jupiter had had Hans and Konrad, over a period of a year, place in such a way that they completely hid the 30-foot mobile home trailer they used as Headquarters.

Mrs. Jones stared at the pile of material and frowned.

"Jupiter!" she called. "Why haven't you boys been listing this material over here?"

Jupiter looked at Bob and he looked at Pete and Pete looked at both of them. No one spoke.

"Jupiter!" Mrs. Jones called. "Do you hear me? Come over and help me see what's here!"

She started tugging away at pipes and boilers, and Jupiter and Pete hurried over. They were afraid that in another minute she'd have Headquarters uncovered.

"Excuse me, Aunt Mathilda," Jupiter said, "but that material is not very valuable. It's hardly worth bothering with."

"Hardly worth bothering with!" Mrs. Jones snorted. "Look how big that pile is! I want to know what's inside there," she said. "Maybe we should just get rid of all this stuff and use the space for something more valuable."

Just then a horn sounded three times, and the big salvage-yard truck, with Konrad at the wheel, came rolling into the yard. Mrs. Jones turned to look and the minute she saw what was on the truck, she forgot about the pile of material that hid Headquarters.

"Mercy and goodness and sweetness and light!" she cried. "Titus Andronicus Jones, what have you bought now?"

Mostly what he had bought was ordinary junk, but perched up at the back end of the truck was an iron deer. It was life-size, with huge antlers.

"Hmph!" Mrs. Jones said. "Well, we can sell it to a collector, I suppose, but I'll bet you paid too much money for it."

"I didn't buy it to sell," Titus said. "I'm going to set it up outside the gate." He hopped down off the truck and gave his wife a squeeze around the waist. "Now I'll have two dears," he said.

It was a pretty terrible pun, but Mrs. Jones giggled, and forgot all about looking into the pile of material that hid Headquarters.

"Mercy and goodness," she said, looking at the sun, "lunchtime. You men must be hungry. Where have you been all morning?"

Without waiting for an answer, she started out of the salvage yard toward their little white house, which stood just outside the walls.

"You boys want a regular lunch, or do you want sandwiches?" she called back.

"Sandwiches, please, Aunt Mathilda," Jupiter answered. "We want to have a meeting."

"Oh yes, your club," she said in a vague way, and kept on going. Jupiter had told her they were starting an investigation firm, but the details hadn't registered very strongly in her mind. She kept thinking of it as a club.

Jupiter went after her to bring back the sandwiches, and Pete and Bob helped unload the truck. Then Bob wrote down a quick tally of everything that was unloaded. Hans and Konrad, the two helpers, did all the heavy work. Konrad took time out to tell the boys what had delayed them.

"We find we be down there where your friend, this boy Carlos, live," he said. "So we run over and give a hand fixing up the house. Got everything nice and tight now. That's a good boy, Carlos. His uncle feeling better, too."

They were glad to hear that Carlos and his uncle were coming along all right. They admired Carlos' spunk.

"Mr. Jones, he see they don't have money," Konrad said. "So he pretend Mrs. Jones make mistake in charging for material. He give Carlos back twenty dollar and seventeen cents. He's smart, Mr. Jones is. Twenty dollar sound like a present. Add on seventeen cents and it sounds hokay."

Then Konrad gave them a big wink.

"Got surprise for Jupe," he said. "Carlos send him present. I get it out of truck."

A present? Pete and Bob looked at each other. What could it be?

Konrad climbed into the cab of the truck and came out with a cardboard box. It was tightly tied with string and there were holes punched in the top. Konrad handed it to Pete.

"Carlos say, don't open it outdoors," he told them. "There's a note inside to explain."

Then he went back to help Hans and Mr. Jones finish unloading.

"Come on, Bob!" Pete said. "Let's go into Headquarters and open it. I have a funny feeling it's something Jupe is going to be awfully happy to see."

They slipped around the stacks of junk until they were back by the printing press. Bob moved aside the old iron grating that led into Tunnel Two and crawled in. Pete followed. They crawled along until they reached the panel, which opened when Bob pushed it in the right spot. Then they both crawled up into Headquarters and turned on the electric lights, which were needed because the things piled around outside the trailer cut off most of the daylight.

First Pete closed the ventilator in the roof.

"No use taking chances," he said, as he cut the string around the box. He opened the cardboard flaps and there, squatting in a corner and looking miserable, was a medium-sized dark bird with a yellow beak.

"It's Blackbeard!" Pete yelled.

There was a piece of paper in the box. Bob picked it up. It had writing on it that looked as if someone had spent a long time trying to get the letters into the right shape.

Dear Señor Jupiter,

   Here is Señor Blackbeard. He come home at din-
ner time. I send him to you. I wish you to have him,
for he is my friend and you are my friend. Besides,
I have fear the fat man try to steal him. We now
have nice house and I thank you one thousand times.

                   Carlos Sanchez.

When Bob finished reading the letter out loud, the mynah bird fluffed up his feathers and hopped onto the edge of the box. He looked at Pete's fingers as if they might be good to eat. Pete jerked his hand away.

"No, you don't!" he yelled. "You tried my ear yesterday. You're not getting any more of my blood. You might turn into a vampire mynah bird."

There was a noise behind them. Jupiter had crawled into Headquarters and started to stand up. He was only halfway straightened up when he came eye to eye with Blackbeard sitting on the edge of his box.

Jupiter and Blackbeard froze. For a moment they stared into each other's eyes. Then Blackbeard flapped his wings.

"I'm Blackbeard the Pirate! I've buried my treasure where dead men guard it ever!" he croaked. "I never give a sucker an even break, and that's a lead pipe cinch!"

And he laughed, in a phony way, like a man who knows a good joke he isn't going to tell.

Chapter 9

Calling All Ghosts

PETE, BOB AND JUPITER sat around the desk in Head-quarters, devouring the sandwiches Jupiter had brought. They knew that as soon as lunch was over Mrs. Jones would be putting them back to work. Over their heads Blackbeard sat in the cage Jupiter had found for him out in the salvage yard, and seemed to listen to every word.

"We know Mr. Claudius has Billy Shakespeare and Little Bo-Peep," Pete argued. "We heard him say he has four of the parrots. We started out to get back Billy and Bo-Peep. So I suggest we just go right to Mr. Claudius and tell him if he doesn't return them we will call the police. He won't know we promised not to, and that we are just bluffing."

"Hmmm." Jupiter pinched his lip. Bob guessed he was thinking about the bigger mystery of what the parrots meant and why Mr. Claudius wanted them so badly. It was pretty plain Jupiter itched to solve that mystery.

"There is a complication," Jupiter said. "It now appears that the mysterious Mr. Silver intended Mr. Claudius to have the parrots in the first place."

"Maybe," Bob put in. "But that didn't give Mr. Claudius the right to steal them from Mr. Fentriss and Miss Waggoner. I vote with Pete. We should go tell him he has to give them back. We'll take Hans or Konrad with us. That'll keep him from acting nasty."

"Very well," Jupiter said. "Here is Mr. Claudius' card."

From his pocket he fished the card that Carlos had given him. It said:

CLAUDE CLAUDIUS
Dealer in Art Rarities
London—Paris—Vienna

Under that was written the address of a big Hollywood apartment house and the telephone number.

"You telephone him, Bob," he said. "He has never heard your voice. Say you have a Yellowhead parrot for sale and wonder if he would be interested. Your mother bought it from a Mexican peddler. Then make an appointment to go see him, and we will, of course, all go together."

Bob dialed. He wondered if he could carry off the story. But as it turned out, he did not have to. The switchboard operator who answered told him that Mr. and Mrs. Claudius had moved from the apartment house two days before.

They could all hear both sides of the conversation, of course, over the loudspeaker Jupiter had made. Now Jupe whispered in his ear:

"Ask if they took their parrots with them."

Bob did so. The reply he received was that Mr. and Mrs. Claudius had had no parrots in their apartment as no pets were permitted in that building. He hung up, looking blank.

"He's gone. Now we don't know where to find him after all."

"Great," Pete remarked. "We're making terrific progress. All backwards."

"A momentary setback," Jupiter observed. "They undoubtedly have another address, where they can keep the parrots unobserved. Of course they would not take stolen parrots into a lavish apartment house. It would be too noticeable."

"All right," Pete said. "I've used up all my ideas. You do the talking now."

"Perhaps Bob has something to say." Jupiter looked across at the smaller boy. "He is very observant of details."

"Also he uses shorter words than you do," Pete muttered. "Okay, Bob, what's your opinion?"

"Well," Bob said, "before we start making new plans, I think we ought to get all our facts in order, so we can see the case more clearly. We got into it in the middle, actually, after Mr. Fentriss' parrot was stolen. But it really started long before that."

"Yo-ho-ho and a bottle of rum!" screeched Blackbeard.

"Go on, Bob," Jupiter said. "It's very helpful to hear the facts presented by someone else."

"It seems to me," Bob said earnestly, "that the case really started with the Englishman who called himself John Silver. When he arrived at Carlos' uncle's house many months ago, he admitted that he was in this country illegally and had run away to avoid arrest back in England. Also, he had with him a flat metal box in which he claimed he kept a valuable treasure he didn't dare sell."

Bob looked over at Jupiter, but Jupiter appeared satisfied to let him talk, so Bob continued.

"Mr. Silver was ill," Bob said. "He was dying. Before he died, he hid his metal box and the treasure, if there was a treasure. But he left behind seven parrots, counting Blackbeard as a parrot, which he had trained to utter strange and baffling remarks."

"Strange and baffling," Pete muttered. "That's putting it mildly."

"He told Carlos and his uncle"—Bob referred to his notes—"to mail a letter, and soon a fat man would come and pay them a thousand dollars for the parrots. But the fat man, Mr. Claudius, didn't come in time. Carlos' uncle sold the parrots to pay for Mr. Silver's funeral. Then, when the fat man did come, he was in a rage because the parrots were gone. However, he set out to try to find them. Knowing the part of town where they were sold, he apparently kept looking until he located four of the parrots. We know he stole two of them, and maybe he stole all four.

"It was because he stole Billy Shakespeare that The Three Investigators got into the case. Now we have

Blackbeard, a bird Mr. Claudius especially wants, and we haven't any idea where the two missing parrots are. Nor do we have any idea why the birds are so important to Mr. Claudius. Mr. Claudius has moved, and apparently gone into hiding, so we don't know where he is. And that"—Bob took a long breath—"is about where we stand now."

"Look under the stones beyond the bones! I never give a sucker an even break!" shrieked Blackbeard, flapping his wings.

"Stated with great clarity," said Jupiter. "But I think I can add a few deductions of my own. To begin with, Mr. Silver was a man who knew books and probably worked around books. First, look at the name he selected for himself—John Silver. I feel sure he borrowed it from the character of Long John Silver, the pirate in *Treasure Island*."

"Well, that makes sense," Pete agreed.

"The very fact that he named himself after a pirate gives us a hint that this mysterious treasure of his was stolen in the first place, which was probably the reason he didn't dare try to sell it.

"To confirm the fact he was a man who worked around books," Jupiter went on, "look at the names he gave the parrots. Billy Shakespeare——Little Bo-Peep——Blackbeard the Pirate——Sherlock Holmes——Robin Hood——Captain Kidd."

"And Scarface," Pete reminded him.

"Probably named after a character in a gangster film.

In any case, most of the names have bookish or historical associations."

"Hey!" Bob exclaimed. "Maybe the treasure he had in that metal box was a rare book. Some rare books are worth thousands of dollars!"

Jupiter frowned.

"That's true," he said. "But remember Mr. Silver's description of his treasure as being 'a piece off the end of the rainbow with a pot of gold underneath it.' That doesn't sound much like a book."

"No," Pete chimed in. "So where does that leave us? We've lost Billy and Bo-Peep and Mr. Claudius. We're up against a blank wall."

"Not totally blank," Jupiter said. "Yesterday we heard Mr. Claudius himself say that two parrots are still missing. I suggest we obtain those two missing parrots. Then, with Blackbeard, we'll have three of the birds and Mr. Claudius will have four. Sooner or later he will learn we have them, and then we won't have to locate him. He will come to us."

"I'm not sure I like the idea of him coming to us," Pete muttered. "And I certainly don't like the idea of going out and stealing parrots."

"I do not propose to steal them," his stocky partner said. "It is my intention to try to buy them."

"Buy them?" Pete demanded, as Bob looked puzzled also. "How can we buy them when we don't even know where they are?"

"You're forgetting the Ghost-to-Ghost Hookup," Jupiter said. "I know at least three boys who live in this section of Hollywood." He put his finger on the map where Carlos had drawn a line around a certain area. "I'll telephone those boys. They in turn will call others, and soon the entire area will be blanketed by inquiries."

Bob and Pete looked impressed.

"Jupe, you've got it!" Bob exclaimed. "Why, a parrot is interesting to everybody. I mean, if a neighbor buys a parrot, and if the parrot talks well, it's the kind of thing people talk about. Everybody on the block will know about it soon. No matter who bought those parrots from Carlos' uncle, someone will know, and the Ghost-to-Ghost Hookup will spot them!"

"We can't offer a reward this time," Jupiter said, "but I feel sure just the excitement of helping in an important investigation will spur our ghosts on to help us."

"How can we buy them if we haven't any money?"

"I shall try to get some money," Jupiter said. "And if I can't, perhaps we can persuade the owners to let us make a tape-recording of what the birds say. Because it is obvious now that before he died, the mysterious Mr. Silver taught the parrots to say certain odd and bewildering phrases for a definite purpose. And that purpose explains why Mr. Claudius is so anxious to get his hands on all of them. I'm sure the reason——"

Just at that moment Mrs. Mathilda Jones's voice came ringing across the salvage yard.

"Jupiter! Pete! Bob! Where are you rascals hiding? It's time to get back to work, do you hear? Back to work!"

They didn't linger—not when Mrs. Jones called like

that. They went out through Tunnel Two like three bullets from one gun. Behind them as they went they heard Blackbeard croaking, "Back to work! Back to work!"

He sounded as if he was enjoying himself.

Chapter 10

Into a Trap

"THIS SEEMS TO BE the first address," Pete said, consulting a slip of paper with two names and addresses written on it. "Stop here."

"You bet," said the man who was driving the Rolls-Royce the following morning. He was a short man with shrewd, inquisitive eyes, named Fitch. When Jupiter had phoned to ask for Worthington and the car, the Rent-'n-Ride Auto Rental Agency had informed him that Worthington was away. That was a disappointment, because the boys were used to Worthington. However, there was nothing to do but agree to another driver.

The car pulled up to the curb and Fitch turned around to grin at Bob and Pete. Jupiter was not with them. That morning his aunt's sister had been taken ill. His aunt and uncle had hurried away, and he had been forced to remain in charge of the salvage yard. Hence Pete and Bob were on their own.

"You kids going to do some detecting today?" Fitch asked. "Worthington was telling me about your setup. Say, anytime you need help, call on me. I was a bank guard once." He tapped his forehead. "Believe me, what I don't know about crooks isn't worth knowing."

Neither of the boys thought much of the new driver. Pete gave a short nod and said, "Thank you, Fitch. However, today we're just going to try to trace some missing parrots."

"Trace some missing——" Fitch began, and his face got red. "Okay, I can take a hint."

He turned around and picked up a newspaper. He thought Pete was joking.

The previous evening Jupiter had put into effect his Ghost-to-Ghost Hookup, as planned, concentrating on that section of Hollywood and seeking information about anyone who had recently bought yellow-headed parrots. Several answers had been received from boys in the area. From the information thus received, they learned that a fat man had been going from door to door several days before, and had located two of the parrots—Captain Kidd and Sherlock Holmes. He had managed to buy them by offering double what the owners had paid for them.

However, the fat man had missed the two parrots named Scarface and Robin Hood. Pete and Bob had the addresses of the people who had bought these two, and hoped to be able to buy them. They had seventy-five dollars with them, money Jupiter had persuaded his aunt to advance them by promising all three would work hard in the salvage yard for at least two weeks. They hoped it would be enough. If not, Pete had his portable tape-recorder with him, and would try to get a recording of whatever odd speeches the birds might have been taught.

Leaving the car, the two boys started up a cement walk between high bushes. They were approaching an old-fashioned stucco house, and were about twenty feet from it when the front door opened and a tall, skinny boy with a long nose stepped out. He grinned at them in a malicious manner.

"Skinny Norris!" Pete exclaimed, as he and Bob stopped in surprise. "What are you doing here?"

E. Skinner Norris spent part of each year in Rocky Beach with his family, who were legal residents of another state. As his home state gave out automobile driving licenses at an earlier age than did California, Skinny was able to drive his own car. Using this advantage and a large allowance, he tried to make himself a leader among the young people in the town.

It was his ambition to show that he was smarter than Jupiter Jones, and he had tried several times to prove it, without success. As a result, he spent a lot of time trying to pry into Jupiter's affairs, and those of his friends. He did not succeed often, but there were times when he could be very annoying.

E. Skinner smirked at them now. He had his hands behind his back, hiding something.

"Aren't you a little late?" he taunted. "That is, if you came for this."

From behind his back he brought a parrot cage. In it sat a parrot with a yellow head. Its right eye was missing, and there was a scar down one side of its head where it had apparently been in a fight.

"A parrot?" Pete tried to act surprised. Bob chimed in to help along the bluff.

"Why should we be interested in a parrot, Skinny?" he asked.

The bluff did not work, though. This time Skinny had them beat, and all three knew it.

"I just happened to be next door last night," he said, gloating over them, "visiting a friend. My friend had a telephone call that Fatso Jones wanted to locate recently bought yellow-headed parrots. He told me there was one in this house, so I came over this morning and bought it for forty dollars. I happen to know where I can sell it for a hundred and fifty. So there's no use my wasting any more of my valuable time talking to you two."

He marched past them, carrying the parrot cage. As Skinny went by, the parrot gripped the bars of his cage and cocked his head.

"I never give a sucker an even break," he croaked.

"Shut up, you!" E. Skinner Norris said furiously, and hurried on down the street. They saw him get into a blue sports car that they hadn't noticed before because it was concealed behind some bushes, and drive off.

"Whom do you suppose Skinny thinks he can sell the parrot to?" Pete asked. "Mr. Claudius?"

Bob didn't have the faintest idea. But he did pull out his notebook and scribble in it.

"I'm writing down what Scarface said," he explained. " 'I never give a sucker an even break.' Even if we don't have the bird it sounds as if we have the message Mr.

Silver taught it. Maybe Jupe can make something of it."

"If he can, he's a wizard," Pete said. "It sounds like something out of an old gangster movie on TV. Well, let's see if we can locate Robin Hood."

He and Bob climbed back into the waiting car and Pete gave Fitch another address. This turned out to be several blocks away. It was an old house, badly run-down, set well back.

As they walked up to it, Pete turned to Bob.

"I've been thinking," he said. "This Ghost-to-Ghost Hookup that Jupe invented for contacting hundreds of kids to get information."

"What about it?" Bob asked. "It's a terrific idea. Almost as good as a radio broadcast."

"That's the trouble," Pete said. "It gets results, but also it lets a lot of people know what you're up to. And sometimes the wrong person is bound to find out something you'd rather he didn't know. Just as Skinny learned we were interested in parrots and got in ahead of us to buy Scarface."

"At least he didn't know about Robin Hood," Bob answered. "This is the house where they bought Robin Hood, or anyway that's what a boy who lives next door told Jupe on the phone. I sure hope we can buy him back."

This time luck, having run against them once, now turned in their favor. The owner of the house, a short man with a bald head, had bought a parrot from a Mexican peddler about three weeks previously. When he bought it, the peddler had stroked it and it had called itself Robin Hood and rattled off a string of words, but it hadn't said a single word since. His wife was disgusted with it and would rather have a canary.

He was glad to let them have Robin Hood for the twenty-five dollars he had paid for it, but as he handed them the cage he warned, "It can talk, but it won't. Just doesn't feel like it. I don't know what you can do about it."

"Thank you, sir," Bob said. "We'll try to get it to speak."

Elated, he and Pete hurried out. True, Robin Hood sat glumly on his perch and didn't act like a parrot who had any intention of talking. But they were sure Jupiter would somehow persuade it.

"We'll go straight back to Headquarters," Pete said, "and see if—— Say, where is the car?"

The car, which they had left at the curb, was nowhere in sight.

"That Fitch!" Bob said. "Going off and leaving us here!"

"Maybe it's his idea of a joke," Pete answered. "But no matter what it is, we're going to have trouble getting back to Rocky Beach."

A rather battered closed-body truck rolled up and stopped beside them. A woman was driving it, and she leaned over to speak to them.

"Are you boys looking for that old Rolls-Royce?" she asked. "It drove away a few minutes ago."

"It was supposed to wait for us," Bob said.

"Oh, what a shame." The woman sounded sympathetic. "Perhaps I can give you a lift someplace. At least to where you can get a bus."

"Thanks a lot," Pete said eagerly. "Come on, Bob, we'll get the bus over at Wilshire."

He hopped into the truck and settled down beside the woman. Bob, holding the cage with Robin Hood in it, followed. For a moment he thought he had heard the woman's voice before. But that didn't seem possible.

"Excuse me, but Wilshire Boulevard is back of us," Bob said, as the woman started the truck off at surprising speed.

"We're not going to Wilshire Boulevard, my fine lads!" a voice with an English accent grated in their ears. "We have another destination."

Startled, Pete and Bob swiveled their heads as a panel in the partition between the seat and the closed body of the truck opened. Mr. Claudius was leaning through it, only inches behind them.

His round fat face had a ferocious smile on it, and his eyes glittered behind the thick glasses.

"You're coming with me this time," he said. "I've had all the interference from you I'll stand for, do you hear?"

The boys were too frightened to speak. They just stared at him. Still smiling, Mr. Claudius brought his hand into view. It held a long, thin dagger with squiggly curves in the blade.

"Now, my boys," Mr. Claudius said, "a single move will be your last. This serpentine dagger was made in

Damascus a thousand years ago. It has a history of having killed twelve people. I'm sure neither of you wants to become the thirteenth. Thirteen is such an unlucky number!"

Chapter 11

Seven Flying Clues

THE TRUCK MADE rapid speed toward the steep and barren hills beyond Hollywood. Neither Pete nor Bob could utter a word.

"I tried to warn you boys," the woman said, at one point. "But you wouldn't take my warning."

Then Bob realized where he had heard her voice before —over the telephone, when she had advised him and Jupiter to stay out of Mr. Claudius' way.

Finally, when they were well out into the hills, Pete got up his nerve to speak.

"May I ask a question, Mr. Claudius? How did you get rid of Fitch and the car?"

"Easily, my boy." The fat man chuckled. "I went to the Rent-'n-Ride Auto Agency to secure a car that wouldn't be recognized as easily as my Ranger. There I discovered the amazing Rolls-Royce you boys had been riding around in. I also learned about the mobile phone in the car.

"Today we followed you here, and while you were in the house I went to a corner store and called the mobile phone. I told Fitch I was calling from inside the house. I said you boys were staying to lunch and he wouldn't be needed before afternoon. So off he went."

"Claude," the woman, apparently his wife, started to say, "don't you think——"

"No, I don't!" the fat man snapped. "Watch your driving. Have you been looking in the rear-view mirror?"

"Yes. At first I thought I saw a small car following us, but we've lost it."

"Good. Watch this turn."

The truck slowed, made a sharp turn, and they were in a long, hollow spot in the hills. A house had been built there, with a two-car garage beside it. The woman drove in and stopped.

"Out, my lively lads, out," said Mr. Claudius. "But don't hurry."

Bob and Pete got out slowly while Mr. Claudius followed. The other half of the garage was occupied by the black Ranger sports car Mr. Claudius had been driving the first time Pete had seen him.

Mr. Claudius led them inside the house, into a big living room that was rather meagerly furnished. At one end four cages holding yellow-headed parrots stood on a big table. The parrots seemed listless and dejected. None of them made a sound—not even when Mrs. Claudius added the cage with Robin Hood to the group.

Bob and Pete sat down on a large couch, and Mr. Claudius sat opposite them, testing the point of the knife with his finger.

"Now, my sly and sneaky scalawags," he said, "I intend to learn a few things. I have five of the seven parrots that

John Silver trained. I shall get the others. Oh yes, I shall.
But at the moment I wish to know, how did Huganay
come to hire you and how much does he know?"

"Huganay?" Pete blinked. Bob looked blank. Who was
Huganay?

"Don't pretend you don't know him," Mr. Claudius
said impatiently. "Huganay, the Frenchman, one of the
most dangerous art thieves in all Europe. I'm positive
he's on my trail."

Bob started to shake his head, but Pete spoke up.

"This Mr. Huganay," he asked. "Is he about medium
height, with dark hair, a French accent, a little moustache?"

"That's him!" Mr. Claudius said. "So you do know
him!"

"We don't actually know him," Pete answered. Then
he described the encounter in Mr. Fentriss' driveway,
when the Rolls-Royce had just missed being rammed, and
told how the man driving the other car had seemed so
interested in the parrot Billy Shakespeare, and how anxious he had been to avoid the police.

"Yes," Mr. Claudius said, "Huganay would be anxious
to avoid the police. But I don't understand. If you are not
working for Huganay, why are you interested in these
parrots?"

As Pete explained how The Three Investigators had
come to meet Mr. Fentriss and promised to help him
recover Billy Shakespeare, all the menace seemed to drain
out of Mr. Claudius. He took off his glasses and wiped

them. A very bewildered fat man started to talk in a quiet voice.

"I was so sure you were working for Huganay!" he said, shaking his head. "The other day when I drove back to my apartment house, I saw Huganay on the corner, watching me. Then, when I entered our apartment, I was certain it had been searched. And I was right!"

He looked at his wife.

"You told me I was imagining it! But Huganay really was on my trail. He had been in my apartment reading my notes!"

"Yes." The woman sighed. "Huganay is after us, there's no doubt. But I'm sure he doesn't know about this place."

"No," Mr. Claudius agreed. "Fortunately," he told the boys, "I had already rented this cottage as a place to bring the parrots. I left the Ranger here and rented an old sedan, one Huganay couldn't recognize so easily. He knows that I love Rangers. Then, the very next day, I heard that you boys were trying to discover the where-abouts of my car. I learned about it from the manager of the building, whose son had asked his father where my Ranger automobile was. His father told him not to pry into the affairs of tenants, so I was safe there."

"I questioned the boys so I could get your number, then I phoned to warn you," Mrs. Claudius said. "My husband was very upset and I was afraid of what might happen if he encountered you again."

"Yes," the fat man sighed. "I have such a terrible

temper when I get upset. I can't control it. I threaten people. And having Huganay on my trail, such a clever and dangerous man"—he passed his hand across his brow —"I've been almost distracted," he said. "And when I ran into you again at Mr. Sanchez' home, I was certain you were working with Huganay."

He seemed to become aware of the deadly-looking blade he held in his hand and he put it down.

"I guess I don't need that," he said. "But now I don't know what to do. I just don't. There are so many problems—so many problems——"

His voice trailed off. He gave a deep sigh. Now his wife spoke.

"Claude," she said, "the time has come to act sensibly. These are clever boys who are not trying to do you any harm. I suggest you apologize to them. You might even ask them to help you. It seems to me they've shown a good deal of intelligence in this matter. They found Mr. Sanchez and they found that parrot when you couldn't." She pointed to Robin Hood, huddled on his perch like the others.

"Yes, you're right," Mr. Claudius dabbed at his face with a large handkerchief. "Boys, may I offer my humble apologies? The trouble with me is my temper. I get so upset when things go wrong, and this matter means so much to me, so very much. I should stay calm. I have a stomach condition that requires me to keep calm. But I just can't!"

Pete and Bob exchanged glances. Bob spoke for both of them.

"We accept your apology, Mr. Claudius," he said. "But what about Mr. Fentriss and Miss Waggoner? You stole their parrots, and you tied up Mr. Fentriss and— well, that's breaking several laws."

Mr. Claudius mopped his face again.

"I shall try to make it up to them," he said. "I shall try very hard, and they will decide whether or not to forgive me. But first I have to explain why I did these things. You see, I stole those parrots because I had to have them. I simply had to! They are tremendously important clues to the priceless treasure which John Silver hid before he died!"

Suddenly Bob understood. Jupiter had been about to tell them his theory the day before. Now Bob could guess what that theory was.

"Mr. Claudius," he asked, "are all seven birds talking clues? Is the speech each one makes a separate clue, and in order to find the treasure do you have to put them all together and figure out what they mean?"

"Yes," Mr. Claudius told them. "John Silver was playing a joke on me, you see. The most fantastic jest of his life. Leaving seven talking birds with cryptic messages for me to solve in order to uncover the treasure he hid! No one else would ever have thought of such a thing. But it was like him, it was just like him. That was how his brilliant but erratic mind worked."

"Claude," his wife interrupted, "the boys will understand much better if you begin at the beginning. While you do so, I will make some sandwiches. I'm sure we're all hungry."

Bob and Pete suddenly realized that they were very hungry. But they were also excited by the knowledge that at last they were going to learn what was behind the mystery of the talking birds.

"You knew Mr. Silver in England?" Bob asked.

"About two years ago," Mr. Claudius said, "I employed John Silver in my business of buying and selling rare objects of art. This was in London. Silver was a highly educated but eccentric man. He could never hold a job long because of his strange sense of humor. At last he was reduced to earning a living by selling jokes, puzzles, and riddles to the newspapers and magazines.

"Then he came to me for a job. He had a wide knowledge of both art and literature. I hired him to attend auctions and buy for me objects that he thought might be valuable.

"One day he brought back a picture. It was a very ordinary picture of two yellow-headed parrots on a branch and he had paid a lot of money for it. Well, as you know, I am excitable. I lost my temper. I called him a fool, and I discharged him.

"John Silver—that was not his real name, but the one he used as a puzzle-maker—told me he was sure the parrots were painted on top of an older and much more valuable painting. He said he would prove it. Perhaps you have heard of one picture being painted over another, sometimes in order to hide the first picture?"

Pete hadn't, but Bob nodded.

"Well," Mr. Claudius continued, "that's what had been

done. John Silver cleaned off the picture of the parrots. In a few days he returned to show me an absolutely lovely little picture of a young shepherdess tending a baby lamb.

"It was obviously by one of the great masters of painting. I knew at once it could not be worth less than one hundred thousand dollars, small as it was."

"Wow!" Pete exclaimed. "That's a lot of money for a painting. I can get them at the store for four ninety-eight with frame."

"Those are just printed copies," Bob told him. "The Metropolitan Museum of Art in New York City paid more than two million dollars once for a picture by the Dutch painter Rembrandt."

"Oh boy!" Pete said in awe. "Two million dollars for a painting?"

"Now we come to the unfortunate part of the story," Mr. Claudius told them. He was interrupted by the arrival of his wife with a tray of sandwiches, two glasses of milk, and two cups of coffee. They all helped themselves, then the man resumed his story.

"John Silver said that because I had discharged him the picture now belonged to him. I told him that he had bought it with my money while in my employ, so it belonged to me. He offered to share it with me, half and half."

"That sounds fair," Pete said. "After all, he found it."

"It was fair," Mrs. Claudius said firmly. "But Claude does fly off the handle when anyone opposes him."

"Yes," the fat man said mournfully. "I threatened John

Silver with arrest. He left with the beautiful picture. I went to the police and swore out a warrant. He fled. Later I learned he had smuggled himself and the picture out of the country on a freighter. The picture, the beautiful shepherdess, was gone."

"You had only yourself to blame," Mrs. Claudius told him.

"Well, boys, I warned art dealers everywhere to be on the lookout for Silver and the painting. But of course, they never turned up. He was, it seems, hiding here in California."

"Yes, sir," Bob agreed. "He was staying with Mr. Sanchez. He was quite ill. He had a flat metal box, and he told Mr. Sanchez that in it he had a piece off the end of the rainbow with a pot of gold at the end of it, but he couldn't risk trying to sell it."

"An excellent description," Mr. Claudius said. "For the picture is as beautiful as if painted with the colors of the rainbow.

"Well, eventually I received a letter from John. It told me that receipt of the letter meant he was no longer alive, but that he had put the picture in a safe place. Finding it, he informed me, would mean solving a riddle. It was his last joke, a joke at my expense, and it had given him considerable pleasure to think it up.

"In his letter he explained that he had trained six yellow-headed parrots and a mynah bird, each to repeat a message. I was to come to America and pay a Mr. Sanchez a thousand dollars for the birds. Then I must make them speak and solve the riddle of their messages before I could find my lost shepherdess. The idea had come to him, he said, because the original picture over which we quarrelled depicted two yellow-headed parrots."

"I guess it was his way of punishing you for the way you treated him," Pete suggested.

"Exactly. But still, no great harm might have been done except for bad luck. As you know, I did not come, and Mr. Sanchez finally sold the parrots. You see, I was away in Japan on a buying trip, and the letter waited weeks for me at my London shop. When I read it, I became very excited and rushed here to California at once. I must have said something in public that came to the ears of Huganay, the art thief, to make him follow me."

He glanced at his wife, and she nodded.

"Huganay can smell an opportunity," she said grimly. "Yes, he's here on our trail and he won't stop at anything."

"But that isn't the worst problem," Mr. Claudius said, biting his lip. "After I found that Mr. Sanchez had sold the parrots, I was almost insane with frustration. Being illiterate, he had no records of whom he had sold them to. But he did show me the general neighborhood on the map, and I started going from door to door, asking if anyone had recently bought a parrot from a Mexican peddler. I managed to find the two named Sherlock Holmes and Captain Kidd.

"The owners agreed to sell them because after the Mexican peddler parted with them, the parrots had sulked and refused to speak a word.

"I kept looking for the others, always in desperate fear someone would find my beautiful painting before I could discover where John Silver had hidden it. Then, the other day, calling at the home of Mr. Fentriss, I saw a yellow-headed parrot through the window. There was no answer to my ring. I was afraid that the owner this time might not sell, and so, rashly and impulsively, I broke in and stole the parrot.

"But he wouldn't talk for me! He wouldn't say a word! I conceived a plan. I returned to see Mr. Fentriss and pretended to be from the police. He not only told me Billy Shakespeare's message, but told me where to find Little Bo-Peep, and informed me that when the Mexican peddler, Mr. Sanchez, had left him, he still had Blackbeard.

"Naturally I was tremendously excited, and I gave myself away. Mr. Fentriss became suspicious. At that moment I saw two boys coming up the path. I dared not be caught. I tied up Mr. Fentriss and gagged him—but loosely, so he could soon escape. Then I intercepted you boys and sent you away. As soon as you had left, I made my escape.

"I immediately went to get Bo-Peep, before Mr. Fentriss could warn Miss Waggoner. The house was empty. I had to steal Bo-Peep, too—I had no choice. I was just leaving through the grove of trees when I saw two boys returning with Miss Waggoner."

"That was me and Jupiter Jones," Pete said accusingly. "Then it must have been you who chucked that piece of tile at us?"

"Yes, yes." Mr. Claudius passed his hand over his forehead. "Please forgive me. I wasn't trying to hurt you, only to frighten you."

"That sort of thing just makes Jupiter more determined," Pete said.

"Of course. But let me finish. I went to see Mr. Sanchez again as soon as I could. In the meantime I had become aware that Huganay was somewhere near so I hid the Ranger and hired the old sedan.

"I wasn't trying to hurt Mr. Sanchez when you arrived, though it may have seemed that way. He was coughing badly and I was trying to help him sit up and ease the spasm. But when you boys entered and attacked me, I had to flee. By now I was sure you were somehow working for Huganay. What else could I think? He was the only other person who could possibly know about the painting.

"I realized I must remain hidden. So next I rented the old truck. In it I could ride around unseen, while my wife drove. I redoubled my efforts to find the birds still missing. This morning, as we drove through that part of Hollywood, we saw your Rolls-Royce and trailed it. It's a very noticeable car."

"Yes, I guess it is," Bob said ruefully. "No one could miss it."

"We parked and watched. We saw your encounter with that tall, thin boy who apparently had obtained Scarface."

"Skinny Norris!" Pete said disgustedly. "He horned in because he's jealous of Jupe and is always trying to get ahead of him."

"He drove away with Scarface in a blue car. Imagine my desperation! I wanted to follow him. I also wanted to follow you. In the end I followed you and let him go. I felt we didn't need him because as he passed our parked truck, the parrot croaked out its message. What did it say, my dear?"

Mrs. Claudius referred to a paper in her pocket.

"It said, 'I never give a sucker an even break,' " she reported.

"An old slang phrase, and most baffling as a clue," Mr. Claudius commented. "But anyway, I followed you, sent away your car by a stratagem—and, well, here we are. And it's all been for nothing—nothing."

"What do you mean, for nothing?" Bob asked.

"I have five of the seven birds," Mr. Claudius said. "And so far I know only the messages Mr. Silver taught Billy Shakespeare and Scarface. The rest won't talk for me. They won't speak. They won't say a thing! And they act as if they never will!"

Chapter 12

A Plan of Action

THE BOYS TURNED to look at the five parrots in their cages. All the birds sat drooping and listless. They certainly didn't look as if they intended to talk.

Mr. Claudius jumped up. He strode over to the birds and shouted at them.

"Talk!" he roared. "Tell me the messages John Silver taught you! Do you hear me? Speak!"

The birds huddled themselves into even smaller bundles of feathers and did not let out a peep.

"That's what he's been doing ever since he recovered the first parrot," Mrs. Claudius told Pete and Bob. "Shouting at them."

"That's probably why the birds won't talk, sir," Bob said. "Parrots are quite easily upset by changes and loud noises.

The fat man resumed his seat.

"I get so impatient!" he groaned. "But what am I to do? Time is running out. Huganay, a very dangerous man, is on my trail, and someone may find my lost shepherdess any time. I'm at my wits' end."

Pete spoke up.

"We know the messages Mr. Silver taught several of the birds," he said. "We can't make head or tail of them. But maybe Jupiter Jones can if you tell him everything you've told us."

"Why don't we write out the messages we already know," Bob suggested, "and see if they give us any clue?"

"That's a very sensible suggestion, Claude," the woman said. "I told you all along these boys could help if you would stop treating them as enemies."

"But what was I to think, my dear?" Mr. Claudius asked. "The evidence . . . Never mind. I am properly sorry. Let us try what you suggest, lads, and if it works, if we find the picture, I shall pay you a reward of one thousand dollars."

"Wow!" Pete exclaimed. "Let's get busy. Bob, do you have your notebook?"

"Right here." Bob pulled out his notebook and a pencil.

"First," Mr. Claudius said, "I can add one more helpful fact. In his letter John Silver not only told me that the message had seven different parts, but he told me in what order the parts were to be arranged. For instance, he taught Little Bo-Peep Part 1, Billy Shakespeare Part 2, Blackbeard Part 3, Robin Hood Part 4, Sherlock Holmes Part 5, Captain Kidd Part 6, and Scarface Part 7."

"That helps a lot," Bob said. His pencil raced for a moment. Then he showed them what he had written on the page he tore from the notebook. He had arranged it in this way:

JOHN SILVER'S MESSAGE (Not complete)

LITTLE BO-PEEP: (Part 1)	Little Bo-Peep has lost her sheep and doesn't know where to find it. Call on Sherlock Holmes!
BILLY SHAKESPEARE: (Part 2)	To-to-to be or not to-to-to be, that is the question.
BLACKBEARD: (Part 3)	I'm Blackbeard the Pirate, and I've buried my treasure where dead men guard it ever. Yo-ho-ho and a bottle of rum!
ROBIN HOOD: (Part 4)	?
SHERLOCK HOLMES: (Part 5)	?
CAPTAIN KIDD: (Part 6)	?
SCARFACE: (Part 7)	I never give a sucker an even break.

"So you see," Bob said, as the others crowded around to study what he had written, "we know four of the seven messages already. We—well, we just happen to know what Blackbeard's message is." He didn't feel he should say at the moment that The Three Investigators had the black mynah bird back in Headquarters.

"And," he finished, "we all heard Scarface when Skinny Norris came out of that house with him. So that's how we stand at the moment."

Mr. Claudius' face quivered with frustration.

"But I can't understand it," he said. "It doesn't tell me a thing. Not anything at all."

"Now, Claude," said his wife, who seemed to be made of sterner stuff than her husband, "the first message, about Bo-Peep losing her sheep, obviously refers to the picture itself. It's a sly reference to the fact that the picture is lost and we must find it."

"Possibly," her husband agreed. "But I can't imagine what he means by telling us to call on Sherlock Holmes."

"Neither can I," said Mrs. Claudius. "Now Part 2, Billy Shakespeare's message—— Boys, are you sure you have this correct? The owner told Claude that Billy said, 'To be or not to be, that is the question.' "

"He thought Mr. Claudius was from the police then," Pete explained. "He didn't want to say that Billy stuttered."

"Stuttered! A stuttering parrot for a clue! Oh no, it's impossible, the message can't be solved," Mr. Claudius groaned.

"We mustn't give up!" Mrs. Claudius said, sharply. "Part 2 is certainly unfathomable. But Part 3, Blackbeard's message, suggests some general region where the picture may have been hidden."

"Where dead men guard it ever," Mr. Claudius said, mopping his face. "It sounds like some pirate island. John Silver always had a fondness for tales of pirates and lost treasure. That's why he adopted that name for his puzzle making."

"It does sound like a pirate island," Mrs. Claudius agreed. "Or perhaps something that could be interpreted along the same general lines. We must all think hard."

"But look at Part 7 of the message, Scarface's speech," Mr. Claudius said. " 'I never give a sucker an even break.' An old American slang phrase that means the speaker does not intend to give a fair deal to someone else. Why, that's as good as an admission that John had no intention of our ever solving this message of his."

"If we could get the three missing parts of the message," Mrs. Claudius said, "they might shed some light on what puzzles us. Without them, I guess we can do nothing."

"Mr. Claudius," Bob said. "I have an idea."

"Yes, my boy?"

"We have Robin Hood, Sherlock Holmes and Captain Kidd right here with us. If we could just get them to talk, we'd have all seven parts of the entire message and then maybe Jupiter Jones could make some sense out of it even if we can't."

"But the birds won't talk!" Mr. Claudius exclaimed. "Look at them! They have no intention of talking!"

It was true. Huddled on their perches, the parrots certainly did not seem in any mood to speak.

"Mr. Sanchez helped Mr. Silver train them," Pete said. "They're used to him. They talked for him when he sold them. I bet he could pet them and persuade them to talk. Then when we have all seven parts of the message, we'll take them to Jupiter and see what he makes of them."

"By George!" Mr. Claudius first smiled, then he began to chuckle. He took the paper and tucked it into the outside breast pocket of his coat. "Of course Mr. Sanchez can persuade them to talk. Why, we'll have that picture in our hands before Huganay even knows what's happening!"

Chapter 13

A Wild Flight

HALF AN HOUR LATER they started out in the truck. Mr. Claudius was driving, and everyone was in a very cheerful mood. Pete and Bob sat in the front seat. The five parrots in their cages were hung from a rod arranged across the inside of the closed truck, and Mrs. Claudius rode back there to tend to them.

It was a good many miles from Mr. Claudius' hiding place in the mountains beyond Hollywood to the house where Carlos and his uncle lived, in the flatlands down the coast, but they expected to arrive by mid-afternoon at the latest.

After they had been winding down the lonely hill road for a few minutes, Mrs. Claudius called to her husband in an alarmed voice from the rear of the truck.

"Claude! I was looking through the window in the rear door. There's a car following us!"

"Following us?" The fat man peered into the rear-view mirror fastened to the front fender. "I don't see any, my dear."

"It's behind a curve—there it is. About a quarter of a mile behind us."

"Yes!" he said. "I see it! A big gray sedan. Are you sure it's following us?"

"I can't be positive," his wife said. "But it certainly looks that way."

"Gray sedan?" Pete asked excitedly. "Let me have a look."

He couldn't see over to look into the outside rear-view mirror. Finally he solved the problem by opening the door on his side and leaning out, with Bob grasping him around the waist.

"I don't see——" he began. Then, "It's gaining on us! And it looks just like the car we met in Mr. Fentriss' driveway!"

"Huganay!" Mr. Claudius groaned. "He's on our trail! What will we do?"

"Keep ahead of him until we come to a town!" his wife said, sharply.

"There's no town for five miles," Mr. Claudius said. "Just these lonely hills. But I'll do my best."

He stepped on the accelerator, and the old truck began to race down the long, winding road through the hills.

It swung around a curve so sharply that both boys were piled into the corner of the front seat. Behind them they heard the parrots shriek with agitation. Mr. Claudius was bent over the wheel, holding on grimly and making the tires scream with every curve they rounded.

They went around one curve and saw a drop of five

hundred feet with only a flimsy guard rail at the edge of the road. The truck skidded along the guard rail and jolted back into the road, as Bob and Pete swallowed hard, their hearts pounding.

"Huganay is right behind us now!" cried Mrs. Claudius. "He's trying to pass us."

"I see him in the mirror," her husband muttered. "I'll do what I can."

He swung the truck to the middle of the road. Behind them a horn blared and brakes screamed. The gray sedan, which had started to pass, fell back. The truck went rocking and swaying down the mountain road, holding to the center, keeping the car behind from passing.

Then up the long slope ahead they saw a big Diesel truck, and they were headed straight for it.

"Look out!" Bob yelled. Mr. Claudius swung the wheel. They gained their own side of the road and rocketed past the truck, getting just a glimpse of the astonished expression on the driver's face.

The gray sedan also swung over to miss the big truck. Then in a burst of speed, the sedan roared up beside them. Bob and Pete, hanging on for their lives, saw three men in the sedan—three men and a boy. Pete recognized the man nearest them, waving to them to stop. It was Huganay. But they both recognized the white face pressed against the window of the rear door. It was a thin, long-nosed face that mingled triumph and fear. It was certainly the well-known, if not well-appreciated, face of E. Skinner Norris.

"Skinny Norris!" Pete exploded. "Wait'll I get him! I'll fix him!"

At that moment, though, it looked as if he would never have the chance. They came to a stretch of the road where on their side a steep slope fell hundreds of feet down to a small stream. And inch by inch the gray sedan was crowding them toward the edge.

"I have to stop. Huganay will kill us!" Mr. Claudius cried, jamming on the brakes. The truck came to a stop inches from the edge, while the sedan stopped exactly beside them, so close that they were trapped. They could not get out either door. On one side the deep gulch yawned under them. On the other, the gray sedan prevented the door from opening.

The well-dressed Frenchman smiled across at them, puffing on a cigar.

"Ah, Claude," he said in feigned good humor. "Fancy meeting you here. America isn't such a large place after all."

"What do you want, Huganay?" the fat man asked. He was sweating and his face was white. "You almost killed us then."

"Nonsense," the other said. "I knew you would stop. I believe you have a cargo of parrots in your truck. I am very fond of parrots, so I am going to relieve you of their responsibility. Adams, go around to the back and get the parrots out of the truck."

"Yes, sir!" The little man who had been driving slipped out and went around to the back, where Mrs. Claudius could be heard protesting.

"Let him have the birds, Olivia," Mr. Claudius called to his wife. "There's nothing we can do."

Pete and Bob could see her passing out the five cages to the small man in the road. They could also see the face of E. Skinner Norris who, now that the danger was past, seemed to be enjoying the triumph. He rolled down the rear window of the sedan so he could speak to them.

"Ha!" he jeered. "Investigators! What a joke you kids are! Actually helping a crook!"

Bob and Pete disdained to answer him. By now Adams had the cages out on the road beside the sedan, but he paused.

"Boss," they heard him say, "these cages will take up room. That kid is in the way."

"Okay, boy," Huganay said, "climb out."

"Climb out?" Skinny Norris looked startled. "But I'm helping you."

"You've finished helping us. Lester, toss him out."

"Sure, boss," the third man in the sedan said. He was a big, ugly bruiser, sharing the rear seat with Skinny. It took him only a moment to send Skinny Norris flying out of the sedan so hard that he almost fell into the road.

He regained his balance and turned to Huganay. His face was almost comical in its dismay.

"But you promised me a five-hundred-dollar reward," he protested, "for tracking this criminal for you and helping you get the parrots back."

"Send him a bill, kid," Adams smirked. He finished putting the parrot cages into the sedan. "Hey, boss, there's one missing. The dark one isn't here."

"It isn't?" Huganay leaned out of the car so that his face was only inches from the pale countenance of Mr. Claudius.

"Claude," he said, and his voice was low and dangerous, "where is Blackbeard? I have to have all seven to have the complete message."

"So you did get into my apartment and read my notes!" The fat man showed a spark of spirit. "That's how you got on my trail!"

"Claude," the other man repeated, "where is Blackbeard? I have to have all seven."

"I don't know!" Mr. Claudius cried. "I haven't seen him!"

"But those boys have." The Frenchman transferred his gaze to Pete and Bob. The man's gray eyes had a peculiarly deadly quality. "They're very clever lads. Tell me, boys, where is Blackbeard?"

"We haven't got him," Bob said defiantly. What he said was true—they didn't have him. Jupiter had him, back at Headquarters.

The gray eyes studied them for a moment, then spotted the slip of paper Mr. Claudius had tucked into his outside breast pocket—the paper on which Bob had written the names of all the parrots and the passages they knew so far.

Mr. Huganay reached over and plucked the paper from Mr. Claudius' pocket.

"You're usually very tidy, Claude," he purred. "So this may be important. If—— Ah!" he studied it with pleasure. "Four of the seven parts. So we do not need Blackbeard. We have the other three parrots now and can un-ravel the complete message at my leisure. *Au revoir,* Claude. See you in London."

The big sedan started up and in a moment was out of sight. Mr. Claudius, whose face was now a pasty color, leaned against the steering wheel and groaned.

"What is it, Claude?" his wife asked. "Are you ill?"

"My stomach again," the fat man gasped. "The pain has come back."

"I was afraid that would happen! We've got to get you to a hospital."

The woman jumped out of the back of the truck, hurried around to the front and slid in behind the wheel, pushing her husband over as gently as possible. Bob sat on Pete's lap to make room. Mr. Claudius groaned and doubled up, his arms wrapped around his stomach.

"It's a stomach condition," the woman told the boys as she started the motor. "At times of great excitement it flares up. He'll have to spend several days in the hospital."

She looked across at the boys.

"Please don't mention what has happened to anyone," she said. "Unfortunately, Huganay is not wanted in this country by the police, and we can bring no charge against him. Publicity would mean that the story of the painting would come out and someone might find it while Claude is in the hospital. Naturally, if you can by any means locate it, his offer of a reward still holds. But don't risk a clash with Huganay. He can be very dangerous—very dangerous."

They had almost forgotten E. Skinner Norris. But now,

before they could start, the tall, thin boy hurried across the road to put a hand on the truck door.

"Wait!" he said. "You're going to give me a ride into town, aren't you?"

Mrs. Claudius gave him a look that made the tall boy cringe.

"Get in," she said sharply. "I want you to tell us exactly how you put Huganay on our trail. You had better start talking—fast!"

"Well," Skinny Norris said, speaking rapidly, "I happened to be walking down the street in Rocky Beach when that car stopped and that Mr. Huganay spoke to me. He asked me if I knew some boys who rode around in an antique Rolls-Royce sedan, which he had traced there by the license plate number.

"I said sure I did"—he gave Bob and Pete an uneasy smile—"that they called themselves investigators but were—were——"

He saw the two boys looking at him and faltered. Pete spoke up.

"Go on, Skinny," he said. "Say it."

"I said you were just some kids playing at being detectives who won the use of the car for thirty days in a contest," Skinny said, hurriedly. "Mr. Huganay asked me if any of you had recently acquired one or more new parrots, particularly yellow-headed ones. I said I'd find out and he gave me a number to call. He said some rare yellow-headed parrots had been stolen, and he would give me a hundred and fifty dollars for any I located. Then he drove off.

"Well, that night I was in Hollywood, and I accidentally learned you really were looking for yellow-headed parrots, and I got the address where there was one. So I got there first and bought it. After I bumped into you there, I hurried to telephone to Mr. Huganay.

"He was very nice. He said he was sure you were helping a criminal engaged in stealing rare parrots, but probably didn't know it. He asked me to follow you, if I could, to see where you went.

"I drove around the neighborhood until I spotted the Rolls-Royce. Then I parked around the corner. I was pretty puzzled when it drove off without you, but then I saw you come out with a parrot and get into this truck. So I followed the truck until I saw where it went. After that I drove to the nearest phone to call Mr. Huganay again. He congratulated me and said to wait for him at the phone, that he'd pick me up and we'd nab the criminal and I'd get a five-hundred-dollar reward.

"He came and we were just in time to see you starting out in the truck, so we followed and—and—well, I didn't know he was a criminal himself."

Skinny Norris had never looked so miserable since Pete and Bob had known him.

"Well, that's the whole story," Skinny said nervously.

"That's enough. I've heard all I need to. Now get out!" Mrs. Claudius shouted. "You can walk the rest of the way."

Skinny slipped out of the truck, trembling.

"Thanks to you, young man, I have to take my husband to a hospital. Thanks to you, a dangerous criminal will find a lost masterpiece." Mrs. Claudius' voice was cold. "You may think about that on your long walk home."

She started the truck. Behind them Skinny Norris stood miserable and forlorn in the road, watching them go. Bob and Pete didn't feel very sorry for him, either.

Chapter 14

The Mysterious Message

JUPITER JONES SAT behind the desk in Headquarters. Opposite him were Pete and Bob. He was scowling in concentration. His partners, having finished telling him about their adventures that day, were sitting back, waiting for him to speak. All three were bushed. Jupiter had put in a long day tending The Jones Salvage Yard. Bob and Pete, though they had been home and had supper, still felt a bit exhausted from the exciting events they had been through.

Finally Jupiter spoke.

"Our gold-plated Rolls-Royce," he said, "twice enabled someone to pick up your trail. This teaches us a lesson. In conducting an investigation, it is unwise to attract notice by our mode of transportation, our appearance, or our conduct."

"Is that all you've got to say?" Pete demanded. "Here we had all the parrots together at last—we were right on the edge of getting the whole message John Silver left telling where he hid the painting—and blooie—it's all gone. Now Huganay has the parrots; he has the clues; and maybe by now he already has the painting, too."

"The parrots must have been very upset by all that happened," Jupiter observed. "I doubt if Mr. Huganay has persuaded them to talk yet."

"But he will," Bob said gloomily. "He didn't look like the kind of man who takes no for an answer. Not even from a parrot."

"Still," Jupiter said, "it gives us a little time."

"For what?" Pete demanded. "We know what four of the messages Mr. Silver taught the birds are, yes. But we need all seven. And we'll never get those parrots back now. Not from that Huganay."

"You're right," Jupiter said at last. "We might as well face it. We didn't get back Mr. Fentriss' parrot. We didn't get back Miss Waggoner's parrot. We didn't help Mr. Claudius get back the painting John Silver hid. We've flopped. Our accomplishments are totally negative."

"We didn't even punch Skinny Norris in the eye," Pete muttered. "He's made himself scarce. Gone out of town for a few weeks to visit relatives, their cook reports. Frankly, I'd say we're stuck, all the way around."

For several minutes they were all silent. At last Jupiter nodded.

"Yes," he said. "I cannot think of any way now to find the missing parrots or learn the three parts of John Silver's message that we still do not know. As you say, we're stuck. Our investigation has proved a dud."

Another silence ensued, broken only by Blackbeard's noisy eating of sunflower seeds. At last Bob sighed.

"If only we could have made Captain Kidd, Sherlock Holmes and Robin Hood talk when we had them all together," he said. "At least we'd have the whole message."

"Robin Hood." Blackbeard cocked an eye down at them. As usual, he seemed to be listening to everything. He flapped his wings.

"I'm Robin Hood!" he said clearly. "I shot an arrow as a test, a hundred paces shot it west."

Three boyish faces turned to stare up at the bird in his cage.

"Did you hear what he said?" Pete asked.

"Do you suppose——" Bob gulped.

"Careful!" Jupiter said. "Don't excite him. Let's see if he'll do it again. Robin Hood!" he said to the mynah bird. "Hello, Robin Hood."

"I'm Robin Hood!" Blackbeard said once more. "I shot an arrow as a test, a hundred paces shot it west." The bird flapped his wings again.

Pete Crenshaw swallowed hard. Even Jupiter looked awed.

"Remember," he whispered. "Carlos said he used to ride around on Mr. Silver's shoulder, while Mr. Silver was training the parrots?"

"And now I remember!" Bob said excitedly. "When we first got him he repeated Scarface's message, 'I never give a sucker an even break'—only we didn't know then it was Scarface's. Mynah birds are sometimes better talkers than parrots and this one seems unusually smart. Do you suppose——"

"We'll try it," Jupiter said. He handed Blackbeard a large sunflower seed.

"Sherlock Holmes," Jupiter said clearly. "Hello, Sherlock Holmes."

Blackbeard responded to the name with the sentences he had heard before. He flapped his wings and said in a strong English accent: "You know my methods, Watson. Three sevens lead to thirteen."

"Write that down, Bob!" Jupiter whispered. The injunction was unnecessary. Bob was already scribbling as Jupiter tried again.

"Captain Kidd," he said. "Hello, Captain Kidd." And he handed Blackbeard another seed. The bird ate it and clicked his beak.

"I'm Captain Kidd," he said. "Look under the stones beyond the bones for the box that has no locks."

"Unreal!" Pete said in awe. "This thing is a tape-recorder with wings! Blackbeard knew all seven of the messages all along!"

"I should have guessed," Jupiter said, sounding vexed, "when he spoke another bird's message the first time—Scarface's message, as Bob reminded us."

Blackbeard was into the spirit of the thing now. As soon as he heard the name Scarface he flapped his wings again.

"I never give a sucker an even break!" he screeched. "And that's a lead-pipe cinch. Ha-ha-ha!"

He laughed as if at some tremendous joke. But the boys scarcely noticed. Bob was writing frantically. After a moment he finished and held out a sheet of paper to Jupiter.

"There," he said. "There are all seven parts of the message."

Pete crowded beside Jupiter and both boys read the following:

JOHN SILVER'S MESSAGE (Complete)

LITTLE BO-PEEP: (Part 1)	Little Bo-Peep has lost her sheep and doesn't know where to find it. Call on Sherlock Holmes.
BILLY SHAKESPEARE: (Part 2)	To-to-to be or not to-to-to be, that is the question.
BLACKBEARD: (Part 3)	I'm Blackbeard the Pirate, and I've buried my treasure where dead men guard it ever. Yo-ho-ho and a bottle of rum!
ROBIN HOOD: (Part 4)	I shot an arrow as a test, a hundred paces shot it west.
SHERLOCK HOLMES: (Part 5)	You know my methods, Watson. Three sevens lead to thirteen.

| CAPTAIN KIDD: (Part 6) | Look under the stones beyond the bones for the box that has no locks. |
| SCARFACE: (Part 7) | I never give a sucker an even break, and that's a lead pipe cinch! |

"That's it, all right," Pete said. "The whole message. Now there's just one thing left, just one teensy-weensy little thing."

"What's that?" Bob asked.

"All we have to do is figure out what the message means," Pete told him.

Chapter 15

Ramble and Scramble

ALL DAY WORKING at the library, Bob moved as though his mind was a million miles away—and it was. He took a book on codes and ciphers from the shelf and looked at it, but learned nothing. However, he hoped that while he was getting nowhere, Pete or Jupiter might be getting some clues. After supper he rode his bicycle hopefully down to The Jones Salvage Yard, crawled through Tunnel Two into Headquarters, and was greeted by blank faces.

Pete admitted frankly that he was no good at secret messages. Jupiter, pinching his lip, called the meeting of The Three Investigators to order.

"I don't know what Mr. Silver's message means," he said. "But some points seem to make sense of a sort. Now for Part 1, about Bo-Peep losing her sheep, I agree with Mrs. Claudius. That refers to the picture of the shepherdess and her sheep being hidden."

The other two nodded their agreement.

"But what about that 'call on Sherlock Holmes'?" Bob asked.

"I wish we could!" Pete exclaimed. "We could use him."

"I don't understand that yet," Jupiter admitted. "Because Sherlock Holmes' message, Part 5, is 'You know my methods, Watson,' which is a well-known phrase from the stories, then, 'three sevens lead to thirteen.' So far that last is totally meaningless."

Blackbeard cocked his head. "Three severns lead to thirteen," he announced.

"It sounded to me as if he said 'severns,' not 'sevens,'" Pete stated.

"That's just the English accent," Bob put in. "Go on, Jupe."

"Well, for Part 2 we come to Billy Shakespeare stuttering a famous quotation," Jupiter said. "That doesn't make any sense to me either."

"Part 3, Blackbeard's own message, sounds like a reference to a pirate island or hide-out," Bob said. "Mr. Claudius said John Silver was very fond of stories of pirate islands and if he could find one or anything that could be thought of as one, he might choose it as a hiding place."

Jupiter unfolded a map. "Here is a map of lower California," he said. "We know from Carlos that Mr. Silver was gone three days. He either walked or hitchhiked someplace, hid the picture in the metal box, and came back. But in three days he could have traveled almost anywhere. Out to Catalina Island. Down to Mexico. Maybe even as far as Death Valley."

"Death Valley!" Pete exclaimed. "There are plenty of dead men's bones in that place! That gets my vote. But can't you just see us searching Death Valley for a box? We'd join the dead men guarding it in about two days!"

"It's just one possibility," Jupiter said. "But it does have promise."

"Part 4 of the message, 'I shot an arrow as a test, a hundred paces shot it west,' sounds like a direction," Bob suggested. "To tell us we are supposed to go a hundred yards west from someplace."

"Sure, but where?" Pete demanded. "The corner of Hollywood and Vine?"

"We've already mentioned Part 5, Sherlock Holmes' speech, and agreed we don't understand it," Jupiter said. "That brings us to Part 6, 'Look under the stones beyond the bones for the box that has no locks.' That again sounds like a straightforward direction."

"As straightforward as two pretzels wrestling," Pete grumbled. "What stones? What bones?"

"He's making it sound like a pirate island again," Bob put in.

"I never heard of any pirates on Catalina Island," Pete said, "and that's almost the only island around here."

"There were a lot of highwaymen during the years of the gold rush," Jupiter suggested. "Perhaps you could call them pirates."

"That's a possibility," Bob agreed. "But what about the final message, 'I never give a sucker an even break'? That certainly sounds as if Mr. Silver is telling us he's fooled us all along, especially as the last half of the message is another old slang phrase meaning something is positively certain. What it adds up to is that John Silver is really saying, 'Even if you solve my message you won't find the picture, and that's for sure.' "

Jupiter's round face was set in a discontented scowl. He enjoyed problems but he hated to be baffled. And at the moment he was thoroughly baffled.

"Well," he said, "I only hope that Mr. Huganay, the art thief, is having as much trouble as we are. Because though we have the message, thanks to Blackbeard, he has the other parrots and will sooner or later get them to talk. And we want to find the lost masterpiece before he does. Our pride as investigators demands it."

For a while they were all silent. Then the First Investigator rose.

"I'll phone you when I have made some progress," he said. "No use getting together before then. Or if you have any ideas, you phone me."

They parted, and Bob and Pete made their way to their homes, where their parents looked slightly surprised to see them home so early.

The following day, Jupiter, helping in the salvage yard, made three mistakes in charging customers. Pete cleaned up the family garage and washed and greased his mother's car, waiting to hear from Jupiter. Bob, at the library, misfiled so many books that finally the librarian sent him home, where he stretched out on the window seat in the living room and stared at the clouds over the nearby

Santa Monica mountains, as if hoping to find an answer written up there somewhere.

He was so quiet, even when his father came home unexpectedly for supper, that Mr. Andrews looked at him somewhat anxiously.

"Something the matter?" he asked, getting out his pipe. "Something bothering you, Bob?"

"It's a riddle, sort of, Dad." It had at last occurred to Bob that possibly someone else might be able to offer a suggestion. After all, his father was considered quite a bright man. He turned on his elbow, looking owlishly earnest with his ruffled hair. "If you wanted to hide some buried treasure so that you could leave a message saying, 'I've buried my treasure where dead men guard it ever,' where would you put it?"

"On Treasure Island," his father said, lighting his pipe. "The one Robert Louis Stevenson wrote about. Or some other pirate island."

"But suppose there weren't any pirate islands around?" Bob persisted. "Then where would you put it?"

His father thought about that, puffing to get the pipe well started.

"Hmm," he said. "There's one other good spot that would fit the description."

"There is? Where?" Bob asked, sitting up now.

"A graveyard," his father chuckled.

"Wow!" Bob went by his father so fast, heading for the telephone, that his Dad almost dropped his pipe. Shaking his head at the excitability of his son, Mr. Andrews went to wash up. Bob meanwhile was calling the number at Headquarters. After a few rings Jupiter answered.

"Jupe," Bob said, keeping his voice low. "You know Blackbeard's message?"

"Yes?" Over the phone Jupe's voice had an expectant ring in it.

"Well, suppose it referred to a graveyard. Dead men would be guarding the treasure there, wouldn't they?"

There was a long silence at the other end. Then Jupiter said, in a rather strangled voice, "Bob, don't go out. I'll call you back later."

All through supper Bob fidgeted, waiting for the phone to ring. The ring finally came just as he was finishing dessert. Bob was at the phone before the second ring.

"Yes?" he said.

Jupiter's voice was tense. "Red Gate Rover. Ramble and scramble," he said and hung up.

Bob hung up also. Wow! Ramble and scramble! That meant to get to the salvage yard as fast as possible, to use the secret back entrance, and to be sure no one saw him.

"Mom—Dad—" he said hastily, "I have to go out. Jupiter needs me. I'll be back by ten. May I? Thanks!"

And he was gone before they could open their mouths.

"Now I ask you," his father said, "what was that about?"

"The boys are trying to locate a lost parrot." His mother smiled. "Bob mentioned it several days ago. I suppose Jupiter has a clue."

"A lost parrot." His father chuckled and finished his coffee. "That certainly sounds harmless enough." Then he looked startled. "But what would that have to do with a graveyard?"

Meanwhile, Bob was pedaling with all his might through the back streets toward the rear fence of The Jones Salvage Yard.

Chapter 16

Bob Becomes a Decoy

BOB AND PETE reached Red Gate Rover at almost the same instant. They wasted no words, each knowing the other had received the same message. They got the gate open and their bikes inside. Then they slid and slithered through the tunnel-like path that led to Headquarters, concealed behind its wall of worthless-looking junk, and crawled into the office.

Jupe was waiting for them, a pile of books, maps and papers on the desk in front of him. His air of badly concealed excitement told them he had news.

"We have to proceed swiftly," he told them. "That's why I sent for you."

"Jupe, you've solved the message?" Bob asked.

"Not all of it. But the beginning anyway. You gave me the clue when you suggested that anything buried in a graveyard would be guarded by dead men."

"It was really my dad who had the idea," Bob said, but Jupe was busy with some books and papers.

"With that hint," he said, "I was able to make some progress. Now, the message that John Silver left has seven

parts. He taught each part to a different bird, but we can
forget the birds. We'll just refer to each part as Part 1,
Part 2, and so on."

"Don't talk so much!" Pete groaned. "Say something!"

"Part 3 of the message tells us that Mr. Silver hid his
painting in a graveyard. Therefore, I reasoned that Parts
1 and 2 should direct us to this graveyard."

"They should," Bob said. "But they don't."

"Part 1 of the message says, 'Little Bo-Peep has lost her
sheep and doesn't know where to find it. Call on Sherlock
Holmes.' Do you notice anything odd about the message?"

"Sherlock Holmes is dead," Pete said.

"Sherlock Holmes is just a character in a book," Bob
said. "We can't call him in on the case."

"That's just it!" Jupe said. "The message doesn't say to
call *in* Sherlock Holmes. It says to call *on* Sherlock
Holmes—call on him at his house. And where did he
live?"

"In London," Pete responded.

"On Baker Street in London," Bob said.

"He lived on Baker Street," Jupiter said. "So to call on
him we'd have to go to Baker Street. But look at Part 2 of
the message. It's a quotation from Shakespeare. 'To be or
not to be, that is the question.' A very famous line. But
the parrot who repeated it was taught to *stutter*. It said
'To-to-to be, or not to-to-to be . . .' Parrots don't stutter
unless they are taught to on purpose. That means we're
especially supposed to notice that 'to-to-to be' business."

"I noticed right off." Pete said. "But nothing happened."

Jupiter wrote something on a sheet of paper.

"Look what happens," he said, "when I write 'Baker Street' and put that 'to-to-to be' after it *this* way."

They stared at the paper with popping eyes. What Jupe had written was:

Baker Street 222 B

"Wow!" Pete breathed. "An address!"

"Of a graveyard?" Bob asked.

Jupe dug into the pile of books for an old atlas of Southern California.

"I went through all the books in our reference library," he said. "There are hundreds of towns in Southern California, and more than one has a Baker Street. However, I finally found that in the town of Merita Valley, which is south of Los Angeles, there is an old graveyard at the corner of Baker and Valley streets. And the address of the service entrance, which leads to what used to be the caretaker's house, is 222 B Baker Street!"

"Great!" Pete said. "How did you ever learn that?"

"By using these reference books"—Jupiter patted the stack of books—"and the telephone. I even found a pamphlet that mentions the graveyard. It's put out for tourists. Listen."

He read to them:

"The ancient graveyard in Merita Valley is among the oldest in California. Now unused and in a state of neglect, it is scheduled for future restoration as a site of historic interest."

Jupiter closed the booklet.

"Merita Valley is only about thirty miles south of where John Silver lived with Carlos and his uncle," he said. "With all of the evidence, I feel sure we have located the place where Mr. Silver chose to hide his painting."

"What about the rest of the message?" Bob asked. "Have you figured that out?"

"No," Jupiter told him. "The rest of the message consists of directions to find the actual spot once we have reached the graveyard. We have to go there to puzzle them out."

"Tomorrow morning?" Pete suggested. "We'll go first thing, in the car."

"Mr. Huganay may be figuring out the message, too, at this very moment," Jupiter told him. "We can't waste any time. We have to go there immediately. With Daylight Saving, we have just enough time to get there, find the hidden painting, and return before it gets dark. Unfortunately, we can't all go. And we can't go in the Rolls-Royce."

"Why not?" Pete wanted to know.

"Because Mr. Huganay may have someone watching us," Jupiter told him. "And the Rolls is a very easy car to spot and follow, as we have learned. So this is my plan——"

He explained it swiftly. Bob protested, but to no avail. At last, recognizing the strength of Jupiter's argument, he gave in. Thus, when the Rolls-Royce arrived at The Jones Salvage Yard a few minutes later, all three of the boys climbed in slowly, giving any unseen watcher every chance to observe them.

The little chauffeur, Fitch, was driving again. He favored them with a yellow-toothed grin.

"Locate any good missing parrots lately?" he asked.

"Several," Jupiter said shortly. "One of them is badly wanted by the police. Now drive us out the gate and go around the salvage yard by the back road. As you go down the back road, drive very slowly but don't stop."

Flushing slightly, the chauffeur turned to his job. The car drove out, with the boys in plain sight. When it turned the corner at the rear of the yard, however, and slowed down, Pete and Jupiter scrambled out.

"Wait for us at Headquarters!" Jupiter yelled, then he and Pete dove through Red Gate Rover before anyone who might have been following could possibly have noticed that they had left the Rolls.

"Well, Master Andrews," Fitch said, sounding sarcastic, "where to now? Got some criminal parrots to track down?"

"No," Bob said, trying not to sound disappointed. "Drive up the coast road for about half an hour, then cut east and come back through the hills. This is just a pleasure ride tonight."

But it was no pleasure ride for Bob, despite his words. He was just a decoy. Pete and Jupiter were having all the adventure.

Chapter 17

The Stones Beyond the Bones

THE SMALLER TRUCK from The Jones Salvage Yard jounced down the bumpy dirt street. Konrad was driving, and Pete and Jupiter sat beside him, staring out.

After the two boys had left the Rolls and entered the salvage yard, they had slipped into the truck. Mr. Jones had already promised Jupiter he could have the use of it, with Konrad, for the evening. Konrad had rumbled out of the yard with it as if on an ordinary errand, while the boys crouched down unseen. Not until they had gone ten miles down the coast did they sit up.

"Nobody followed us, Jupe," Konrad said. "And it looks like we found the town you wanted. Not much of a town, huh?"

It had taken them over an hour to arrive in Merita Valley. As Konrad said, it wasn't much of a town. The tiny business section was already behind them. Now they were bumping down Baker Street, which had almost no houses on it. Opposite them was a long stone wall. Behind the wall were hundreds of stone crosses and monuments. They had reached the Merita Valley graveyard.

Pete pointed. There in the wall was an opening, and an old wooden sign attached to the wall read: 222 B Baker Street.

"Aren't you going to stop?" Pete asked. Jupiter shook his head.

"Turn right at the next street, Konrad, please," he said.

"Hokay, Jupe," Konrad agreed.

The graveyard was a large one, and appeared very old. As they came to the corner of the wall, they saw the tumbled-down ruins of a church, built of stone and adobe. It looked deserted and neglected.

Konrad turned the truck, and they kept on for several hundred yards more. Finally, they left the graveyard behind them and came to a large clump of eucalyptus trees beside the road, their branches hanging low, their leaves giving off a pungent, oily smell.

"Park under the trees, please," Jupiter directed. Konrad did so. The boys slid out of the truck.

"We may be gone quite a while, Konrad," Jupiter said. "Just wait for us."

"Hokay," the big man said. He turned on a small radio and got out a newspaper. "I got no hurry."

"Now what, Jupe?" Pete asked as the stockily built First Investigator led them back across an open field, angling toward the crumbling stone wall around the graveyard.

"We don't want to be seen entering the cemetery," Jupiter said. "Our intentions are perfectly respectable, but we don't want any curiosity seekers hampering our hunt."

They came to the wall and climbed over it.

"I don't think I'd mind a little company," Pete said as they started down an untended path. Many monuments, small and large, some of them leaning badly and in sad disrepair, crowded close together on either side.

"You're very good at judging direction, Pete," Jupiter said. "Remember our route so we can find our way back to the truck if the hunt takes us until dark, will you? Unfortunately, we came in such a hurry I didn't bring a flashlight."

"Until dark?" Pete gave a slight yelp. "Anyway, we're not going to have until dark," he concluded as a wisp of vapor brushed across their path. "Look at that! There's a fog rolling in from the ocean tonight."

Jupiter looked toward the west, where the Pacific Ocean lay. It was certainly true that light streamers of fog were slowly rolling toward them. In Southern California fog frequently comes in from the ocean and blankets the areas near the coast, sometimes reducing visibility to almost zero.

"I hadn't counted on a fog," Jupiter said, scowling. "That's even worse than darkness. Let's hope we can unravel Mr. Silver's message swiftly. Anyway, there's the side entrance, the one marked 222 B Baker Street."

Jupiter put on more speed. They passed between two large monuments and came out at an intersection just inside the entrance. Several paths led into the large, old graveyard in different directions.

"What do we do now?" Pete asked nervously as Jupiter took a paper from his pocket.

"We have arrived at 222 B Baker Street," Jupiter said,

peering at the paper. "Part 4 of the message says, 'I shot an arrow as a test, a hundred paces shot it west.' Now, the entrance here faces to the north. Therefore——"

"Therefore what?" Pete demanded. Jupiter was turning around in the center of the intersection of the paths.

"A hundred paces would be equal to a hundred yards," he said. "I'm sure Mr. Silver means for us to go one hundred yards west, and the natural place to start from would be here, where the different paths intersect just inside the gate. So let's pace off one hundred yards. You do it, your legs are longer."

Pete began to stride toward the west, which took them on a path parallel to one wall of the old cemetery, about forty feet in. He made his paces as long as he could. After counting one hundred, he stopped.

"All right," he said. "Now what?"

"Now we come to Part 5 of the message, which says, 'You know my methods, Watson. Three sevens lead to thirteen.' "

"So far it's been easy. But that certainly doesn't make any sense," Pete said.

Nothing in sight gave Jupiter any inspiration. Then a thought struck him.

"Pete," he asked, "are you sure your paces were a yard long?"

"Well—I think so. I stretched all I could."

"Still, let us measure. It always pays to make certain. Take two steps and mark the beginning and end."

Pete did so. His partner took from his pocket a small piece of plastic. This was a calendar for the next three years and along one edge was an inch rule four inches long. With this he measured Pete's paces.

"You've been pacing thirty-inch yards," he announced. "We're fifty feet short of a hundred yards. Take twenty more paces west."

Pete paced westward twenty more steps. This brought them to within sight of the rear wall of the cemetery. But, though there were many commemorative stones around them, he saw nothing that inspired any bright ideas.

Jupiter, however, gave a muffled shout.

"Look!" he said and pointed to three old headstones in a small plot opposite them. The headstones said that Josiah Severn, Patience Severn and Tommy Severn had all died of yellow fever on the same day in 1888, and were here resting in peace.

"Severn!" Pete shouted, as realization struck him. "I told you the message sounded like 'Three Severns lead to thirteen'!"

"Here are three Severns," Jupiter admitted. "But how can they lead to thirteen?"

"Follow the line of the headstones!" Pete said breathlessly. "See if that leads to anything. And golly, we'd better hurry. The fog is coming in fast!"

The fog was swirling all around them now. Visibility was diminishing swiftly. Without wasting time, Pete hurried over to crouch down beside the nearest of the simple markers. The other two stones leaned slightly. Looking directly over the top of all three, he drew a line with his eye that ended at a tall stone marker about fifty feet away.

"The line ends at that stone, Jupe," he said. "See what it says."

Jupiter was already hurrying toward the stone, being careful to step around the old graves out of respect for those who rested there. Pete dashed after him. They reached the tall stone together. It was blank. But when they moved around it, they stopped simultaneously. For the inscription on the other side read:

Here Lie
13
Nameless Travelers
Struck Down
by
Indians
June 17, 1876

"Thirteen!" Pete breathed. "Three Severns led us to thirteen all right. Quick, Jupe, what's the rest of the message?"

"Part 6 says, 'Look under the stones beyond the bones for the box that has no locks,' " Jupiter told him.

"But what stones?" Pete asked. "This whole place is full of stones."

"The message says 'beyond the bones,' " Jupiter retorted. "So it can't mean any of the monuments. Golly, this fog is getting bad. But look, over there, straight beyond this monument and against the wall. There's a pile of stones where a section of the wall has fallen down and has never been repaired. Those are certainly stones *be-*

yond the bones. And they're the only such stones in sight. If we look under them——"

Pete hardly waited for him to finish. He was already galloping toward the collapsed section of wall where hundreds of stones, large and small, lay in a heap. As soon as he reached it, he began grabbing stones, moving them, and looking beneath them.

"Come on, Jupe, give me a hand," he gasped. "We haven't got much time. This fog is going to be a zinger."

Jupiter joined him and both boys started lifting stones from the center, putting them into a new pile farther from the wall, and going back for more. They were burrowing deeper and deeper into the heap of stones when they heard a voice with a French accent behind them.

"I do like to see boys who don't mind working," the voice said.

They looked up from where they were working, crouched over the pile of stones. Out of the swirling fog came the debonair Mr. Huganay, followed by his two henchmen, Adams and the big bruiser, Lester.

"However," the art thief said, smiling down at them, "I think it is now time for us to take over. Men—grab them!"

Pete and Jupiter, coming to the same decision at the same moment, both bolted to get past the three men. Unfortunately, they had no time to coordinate their effort. Pete bumped his partner and both sprawled on the ground. With almost no effort Adams grabbed each by a wrist, twisted each boy's wrist behind his back and forced them to their feet.

"Good!" The Frenchman smiled at them. "Hold them there, Adams. You, Lester, dig into those stones until we find the pretty shepherdess. Then our hunt will be over and you will have earned the bonus I promised you for assisting me."

The big, ugly man went to work with a will, tossing rocks from the pile as if they were pebbles.

Helpless and seething with rage and disappointment, Pete and Jupiter could only stand and watch.

Chapter 18

Hide and Seek in the Fog

THE FOG WRAPPED cold, clammy arms around them as Lester dug into the pile of rocks. He worked with the energy of a dog digging for a bone. He tossed behind him small rocks, bits of tile, a length of pipe, a broken tree branch and assorted pebbles, some of which hit Adams, who objected loudly.

"Watch it, watch it!" Adams said.

"A little less energy, a little more thoroughness, Lester," Mr. Huganay said, standing by and watching.

Pete and Jupiter, still held in Adams' vice-like grip, were forced to watch also, bitter with the knowledge they had come so close to the treasure only to be overtaken at the very end by the clever European art thief.

"Don't feel so badly, boys," Huganay said, seeming to read their thoughts. "I have, after all, outwitted the guards at the Louvre, in Paris, and at the British Museum in London. As it is, you very nearly outsmarted me. That stratagem of sending off your conspicuous old car to be followed while two of you came here by truck was most ingenious."

He chuckled and relighted his cigar, which had gone out in the dampness. The fog wrapped around him like a cloak and the flame of his lighter gave his face a sinister, satanic look.

"I was having you watched, of course. My man phoned to report the Rolls-Royce was leaving with all three of you and he would follow. Twenty minutes later he telephoned to say he had passed the car, and only one of you was in it. He had lost you. I knew then that you were opponents worthy of me, and that I had best act rapidly."

He puffed smoke. Lester was still burrowing into the pile of stones, moving the big ones, tossing out all the small stuff heedless of where it went.

"I had, of course, solved the first part of John Silver's ingenious message," Huganay told the two boys. "But I had not located this dismal old graveyard. Forced to think fast, I telephoned the Tourist Bureau. They keep lists of all such spots for the benefit of tourists, and they were able to tell me where there was a graveyard with the address of 222 B Baker Street. I came swiftly, and just in time, too."

Another stone tossed back by Lester hit Adams. The smaller man growled an oath.

Huganay called to the big man. "Move a bit to one side, Lester. Silver was ill. He'd never have bothered to dig so deeply into a pile of rocks."

Lester obeyed, and a moment later gave a shout of triumph. He wrenched something from under a rock and handed it to Huganay.

"Got it!" he said. "There's your box, Mr. Huganay!"

"Ah!" Huganay said. He took the flat metal box, about fourteen inches wide by twice as long. The lid was secured by a small but stout padlock. "Just the right size," he commented. "Good work, Lester."

"That's the box Carlos said Mr. Silver used to keep under his mattress," Jupiter whispered gloomily to Pete.

Meanwhile, the art thief was busy. From his pocket he took a powerful pair of clippers. One pressure cut the metal. The lock came off, and the Frenchman prepared to open the box.

"One glimpse only, in this miserable weather," he said. "A fine old painting such as this must not get damp."

He opened the lid and gave a cry of rage. Lester crowded close beside him to see what had angered him so. Even Adams tried to see, shoving the boys ahead of him.

"There's just a piece of paper here," Huganay said, breathing heavily. "It says, 'Sorry, my dear fellow, but you didn't study your clues well enough.' "

"Okay, Jupe!" Pete whispered as the boys felt Adams' grip relax slightly. They jerked away together. Pete, who was being held by Adams' left hand, broke free. Jupiter could not.

Pete tumbled backwards to the ground and Adams turned toward him, jerking Jupiter around painfully. Pete felt his hand touch something long and hard and he grasped it. He leaped to his feet and swung the length of pipe his hand had touched. It crashed against Adams' shoulder, and with a howl of pain the man released Jupiter.

Still holding his weapon, Pete grabbed Jupiter's arm

and pulled him along as he dove into the thickest part of the fog, where he could just make out a clump of eucalyptus trees. In an instant they were behind the trees, cloaked in the gray veils of the fog, while behind them the three men shouted conflicting orders.

"They'll be after us in a second," Pete whispered into Jupiter's ear. "The truck is that way."

He pointed. Jupiter just shook his head. To him, in the fog, all directions now looked alike.

"How do you know?" he asked.

"I just know," Pete said. Jupiter believed him. When it came to finding directions or following trails, Pete was an acknowledged expert. Even at night he could keep a direction by some kind of inner sense, where Jupiter, even by daytime, could easily get lost.

"Now listen," Pete said rapidly. "There are clumps of eucalyptus trees planted across this place, all the way to the wall where we entered. Duck from one clump to the other."

"I'll get lost," Jupiter said glumly.

"I'll go first," Pete told him. "I'd stay with you but those three are coming this way and I have to lead them on a false trail. You just keep hunting for trees. When you find one, look for our secret symbol chalked on it, and an arrow pointing the right direction. Then you'll know you're okay. Go that way first!"

He propelled his stocky partner into the fog with a shove. Then he started off in another direction, shouting loudly for the men to hear. "Come on, Jupe, stick with me. We have to go this way."

The voices of the three men, which had been moving toward the boys, changed direction as they followed the sound of Pete's voice. Jupiter stumbled forward, barking his shins on many low monuments, until he found himself in another clump of trees.

Here he paused and listened.

There was a dim light around him. It was almost like being under water. It was impossible to see more than a few feet now and the fog was rolling by in waves, heavy and gray. He looked up. Above him the visibility was slightly greater. He could see, forty feet away, a vague mass that might be treetops. He stumbled in that direction.

Now the voices of the men were scattering behind him, one going this way, another that. It was obvious they were lost. As for Pete, there was no telling where he might be.

Jupiter reached the trees he had seen and peered closely at them. On a smooth section of bark on one he saw a question mark drawn in blue chalk, with an arrow underneath it pointing off to the left.

The question mark was the symbol of The Three Investigators. Each of the three boys carried a different colored piece of chalk to use in placing the mark when he desired to leave a wordless message for the others.

Pleased at himself for thinking up this device, Jupiter moved cautiously in the direction show by the arrow.

He came to another clump of trees, another question mark and another arrow. Anyway, Pete was still moving forward. Behind him, Jupiter heard a cry of pain as one of the men apparently fell over something. Their voices were steadily becoming farther away.

Still the fog thickened. Everything was distorted, as in a bad dream. The branches of trees became arms with claws reaching for him. Ordinary monuments turned into squat creatures barring his path. Tall shafts were towering monsters looming over him.

The stocky boy found himself breathing hard when he finally saw the low outline of the wall in front of him. Then a shape towered up on the other side of the wall. It reached for him, and this time it was alive. Jupiter jerked back.

"It's just me, Pete!" the figure whispered. "Come on, grab my hand and let's make time."

Humbly—and Jupiter Jones was not often humble, it must be confessed—he let his partner help him over the wall and lead him through the dense fog until they reached the truck, the headlights making cones of yellow in the mist.

"You hokay, kids?" Konrad demanded as they climbed into the front seat of the truck.

"Just get us back home, Konrad," Jupiter gasped. "Drive inland and find a route out of the fog."

"You bet." Konrad started the truck and with great caution drove them eastward until the coastal fog thinned and they were in the clear. Then he turned north and headed for home.

Chapter 19

Blackbeard Has the Last Word

FOR A LONG TIME, as they rode, the boys were silent. Finally Jupiter said, "At least the fog will keep Mr. Huganay from following us."

"Why should he follow us?" Pete demanded. "We haven't got the picture."

"He may think we have." Jupiter was pinching his lower lip. "That was a surprising development, finding the box with nothing in it but that note from John Silver."

"If they come after us now," Pete said, "we'll have Konrad and Hans around to help handle them." He swung the piece of pipe which he had gripped firmly ever since he picked it up. "I might get a chance to use this again," he said. "That Adams won't forget the crack I gave him."

"You acted as I knew you would," Jupiter said. "With bravery and perfect timing." Pete didn't answer, though he glowed a little inside. Praise from Jupe was rare, and when it came, it meant a lot. Jupiter, however, was already thinking of something else.

"We solved the message," he said. "The presence of the box proves it. Yet the picture wasn't in the box."

"Part of the message was, 'I never give a sucker an even break,'" Pete reminded him. "That proves Mr. Silver was up to some more funny business."

"Maybe," Jupiter agreed. He spent the entire remainder of the trip thinking and Pete did not attempt to interrupt him.

Before they reached Rocky Beach, they had to pass through fog again, but it was not as thick as it had been farther south. They reached The Jones Salvage Yard without incident.

"Let's get into Headquarters," Jupiter suggested, after Konrad drove off to put the truck away. "We should give Bob a full report."

They used Easy Three to get into Headquarters this time, since no one was watching. Easy Three was a big oak door in its frame which seemed to be leaning against a pile of junk. But when unlocked with a rusty iron key taken from a pot of rusty metal where it would never be noticed, the door led into a huge old boiler which in turn led to a small door into Headquarters.

Bob Andrews was sitting, restlessly reading, as they crawled in.

"Did you find it?" he shouted.

But immediately he knew the answer. Their disheveled and weary appearance, and the fact that they carried nothing except the length of pipe Pete had retained for a weapon, told him something had gone wrong.

"Mr. Huganay caught us," Jupiter said, slumping into his chair.

"But he didn't get the picture either," Pete added, taking his seat. "He found the box but there was just a note in it saying that he hadn't studied the clues well enough."

"Wow!" Bob said. "That's weird. You mean Mr. Silver was playing a sort of double joke? Pretending he'd hidden the picture when he hadn't?"

"I wish I knew," Jupiter said glumly. "I don't think so. The note in the box said, 'Sorry, old man, but you didn't read your clues well enough.' That means there's something in the clues that we missed and Mr. Huganay missed, too."

"I told you . . ." Bob began. Then he forgot what he was going to say because at that moment the phone rang.

They looked at it. They weren't expecting any calls.

"It might be from Mrs. Claudius," Jupiter said, after the telephone had rung five times. "I suppose I had better answer it."

He picked up the receiver and held it near the speaker that allowed them all to listen.

"Hello," he said. "The Three Investigators, Jupiter Jones speaking."

"Congratulations, young Jones," said a man's voice with a small, ironic chuckle, and all the boys looked at each other. It was definitely a voice with a French accent. Mr. Huganay!

"Who is this?" Jupiter asked. He knew perfectly well

who it was, but he wanted a little time to get prepared for whatever threat the art thief might be prepared to utter.

"This is the gentleman you met a little while ago in the fog in a picturesque spot in Merita Valley," said Mr. Huganay's voice. "I just wanted to tell you I have finally figured how John Silver fooled me. It was very smart of you to see what I missed. So—I am abandoning my chase. I know when I am beaten.

"I am at the airport. I will be catching a plane for a foreign country when I hang up. So you cannot catch me. This is just a last-minute salutation from one sportsman to another. Tell Claude I wish him luck with the shepherdess."

"Thank you," Jupiter said, though he had not the faintest idea what the Frenchman was talking about.

"You outmaneuvered me," said Mr. Huganay. "Few people have done that. If you boys ever come to Europe, look me up. I will show you the French underworld and perhaps you may have a chance to try your wits on some mystery there. No hard feelings on my part, if there are none on yours. Agreed?"

"Well—yes," Jupiter said, blinking at his partners. "Agreed."

"Oh—one last thing," Mr. Huganay told him. "I have the parrots in a garage at 89958 Ocean Street, in Santa Monica. You will want to rescue them, I am sure. I have no time to return to see them, so this task I leave to you. *Au revoir,* then, and again my congratulations."

He hung up. Jupiter hung up, too, and the three partners stared at each other.

"Did you get that address, Bob?" Jupiter asked at last.

"Yes," Bob said. "So we can get back Billy and Bo-Peep and the rest, it looks like. But, boy, what did he mean by saying we outmaneuvered him?"

"All I did was slug Adams, grab you, Jupe, and run for it," Pete said. "If that's outmaneuvering him, why—" He broke off. "What is it?" he asked. "Why are you staring at me like that?"

"What," Jupiter asked, sounding slightly breathless, "what was Part 6 of the message?"

It was Bob who answered. "Look under the stones beyond the bones for the box that has no locks," he said.

"Sure," Pete agreed. "And that's where that bruiser Lester found Mr. Silver's metal box, all right."

"But he found a box with a lock on it!" Jupiter exclaimed. "Mr. Huganay had to cut the lock off. And the message distinctly said to look for the box that has no locks."

"That's right!" Pete exclaimed. "There must have been another box. . . . No," he added, "that couldn't be. That was a big box, even if it was flat. If there had been another box, Lester would have spotted it."

"But suppose it was a little box?" Jupiter said. "A small box that didn't even look like a box. What was Part 7 of the message?"

" 'I never give a sucker an even break,' " Pete answered. "We heard Scarface say it himself, didn't we, Bob?"

"That's right," Bob said. "But Blackbeard added, 'And that's a lead-pipe cinch.' I have all of that in my notes, remember? The second half of the message is just a very old slang expression meaning something is positively certain."

"Is it?" Jupiter asked. "Or is the first part of the message really intended to distract our attention, while the last part of the message is there to focus our attention on some very insignificant object, if we are smart enough to read the clues well enough?

"What," he finished, "is that thing on the desk in front of you, Pete?"

Pete looked at it. Bob looked at it. Even the drowsy Blackbeard stuck his beak through the wires of the cage and looked at it.

"It's a piece of pipe," Pete said.

"Where did you get it?"

"I picked it up back in the graveyard and whammed Adams with it," Pete said.

"And it was there because Lester found it under the rocks and tossed it out, right?" Jupiter demanded.

Pete swallowed and nodded.

"Right," he said. "And—it's lead pipe."

"Lead pipe is rather uncommon these days," Jupiter said. "But look at it. The ends of the pipe have caps tightly screwed down, so nothing can get in—no dampness, for instance."

"That piece of pipe," Bob said in a low voice, "with the caps closing it that way, might even be called a box."

"Without," Pete finished for him, "any locks."

"A box without any locks," Jupiter said. "A box that won't rust, won't let in moisture or water or dirt or insects, a box that will last without damage for a hundred years, if necessary. A perfect place to hide something valuable. And we brought it with us!"

Pete was already trying to unscrew the caps on the end of the piece of pipe, which was about fourteen inches long.

"They're on too tight," he said. "I'll get some pliers from the lab."

He was into the tiny lab, which was part of Headquarters, and back so swiftly he hardly seemed to have moved.

"You open it," Jupiter said. "You picked it up."

The boys hardly breathed as Pete applied the pliers to the metal caps on each end of the pipe. They came off after a few turns. Pete pushed his finger into the pipe. As he pulled it out something emerged and fell onto the desk. It was a length of canvas, rolled up tightly.

"Canvas," Jupiter said in a choked voice, "can be rolled up without damaging it, thus a large piece can be kept in a small cylinder. Unroll it, Pete."

Pete unrolled it. He held it out flat on the desk and they all stared at it.

It was about fourteen inches wide by about twenty-four inches long. On the canvas was a painting that even they, untrained in art, knew was rare and beautiful. It showed a young girl, in the costume of a shepherdess, tending a tiny lamb that had injured its leg. The colors were undimmed, glowing with brilliant life.

They had recovered the lost masterpiece.

"A piece off the end of the rainbow," Jupiter said.

"That's how John Silver described the painting. Now I know what he meant."

At the words "John Silver" and "painting" the sleepy mynah bird stirred. They seemed to wake some recollection in his mind. He flapped his wings twice and spoke.

"John Silver," he said. "Good work, good work."

Then the unusual mynah bird tucked his head under his wing and went to sleep. But with the painting on the desk in front of them, the boys could not help feeling that they had just heard a dead man speak to them, and a ghostly chuckle seemed to fill the small space for a long moment, even after Blackbeard went back to sleep.

Chapter 20

In Which Loose Ends Are Tied

WHEN BOB, PETE, AND JUPITER walked into Hector Sebastian's living room two days later, they found the popular mystery writer buried in a newspaper. Realizing he had visitors, Mr. Sebastian looked up and waved them to chairs.

"So you guys are heroes again," Mr. Sebastian said. "I tip you off to a missing parrot and instead you find a lost masterpiece and get your pictures in the paper."

"Only in our local paper," Jupiter said modestly. "The big Los Angeles papers just mentioned that some boys had found the picture under a pile of rocks in the Merita Valley graveyard."

"They didn't even mention The Three Investigators," Pete added.

"But get a load of this," Mr. Sebastian said, holding up the *Rocky Beach News*. "A picture of you, Jupe, and the car you won in the contest. A picture of all three of you holding the painting you found. And a headline that says: 'Three Young Local Sleuths Find Lost Masterpiece.' That's great publicity for The Three Investigators."

"Yes," Jupiter agreed. "We've been offered several assignments already on the strength of that story. What do we have booked, Bob?"

Bob whipped out his notebook.

"Let me see," he said. "A lost Siamese kitten; a statue of the Greek god Pan, stolen from a garden in Hollywood; a ghostly old boat that appears only on foggy nights and always comes ashore in front of a certain house at Malibu Beach; and the mystery of why someone keeps changing the numbers on the front of three houses in Rocky Beach. That's all so far."

Mr. Sebastian looked amazed. "It looks like you guys will be in business for a long time. But let's get back to this case. Tell me the details that didn't get into the papers. Why isn't there a word about Malcolm Fentriss' parrot in the newspapers?"

"That was because Mr. Claudius didn't want to bring the parrots into it," Jupiter said. "He was afraid it might sound too fantastic. Besides—but I'd better start at the beginning."

He proceeded to tell how the investigation had spread to include seven talking birds and a lost masterpiece. Mr. Sebastian listened attentively.

"So," he said, "in the end you got back the parrots, decoded the mysterious message, and found the painting, which you returned to Mr. Claudius."

"That's right," Jupiter said. "Of course"—the admission came with some reluctance, but Jupiter was too honest not to make it—"we did have some luck."

"Luck," Mr. Sebastian said, "helps only when you know

how to use it. Am I right in assuming that you've given Billy Shakespeare back to Malcolm and Little Bo-Peep to Miss Waggoner?"

"Yes, you are," Jupiter said. "They were both delighted to get their pets back. Mr. Claudius explained everything to them and apologized for the way he acted. They agreed to forgive him."

"Well," the writer said, "it will be my pleasure to introduce this case for you—and any other cases you solve."

"Thank you, sir!" Jupiter cried, and Bob and Pete echoed the words. The First Investigator leaped to his feet. "Come on," he said. "We have to get busy."

There was a flurry of boys, and then they were gone.

"Mmm," Mr. Sebastian murmured to himself, "I wonder if I should have told the boys about my friend Professor Yarborough and the ancient mummy that he says whispers to him whenever he's alone in the room with it."

The mystery writer settled back in his chair again and puffed thoughtfully on his pipe.

Hector Sebastian
Speaking

There are a few details in *The Mystery of the Stuttering Parrot* that need wrapping up. Since the Three Investigators are busy on the trail of their next case at the moment, I'll do the explaining.

Mr. Claudius, the fat man, returned to England with the long-lost masterpiece that The Three Investigators had recovered for him. He wanted to give the boys the thousand-dollar reward. But Jupiter insisted he give the money to Carlos and his uncle Ramos, who had sheltered John Silver.

Carlos' uncle went back to Mexico with the money, where he's getting his health back in his native village. The boys introduced Carlos to Worthington, who was so impressed by Carlos' knowledge of automobiles that he took him down to the Rent-'n-Ride Auto Rental Agency. The manager gave him a job washing and polishing the company's cars. Carlos is learning how to be a mechanic in his spare time. He's totally happy working with cars. He lives with the Joneses and pays for his board by doing odd jobs in the salvage yard one day a week.

Mr. Huganay, the tricky art thief, is still at large in Europe, though the police of several countries are trying hard to nab him. Adams and Lester, the thugs he hired, got an unpleasant surprise. Huganay left the country without paying them anything. That convinced them that crime is a losing proposition.

Well, that does it for *The Mystery of the Stuttering Parrot*.

During my years as a private detective I learned to trust my hunches. And I have a strong hunch now that The Three Investigators' next case will be as intriguing and mystifying as this one was. So keep on the lookout for Jupiter, Bob, and Pete because even now they're tracking down fresh clues.

THE THREE INVESTIGATORS MYSTERY SERIES

NOVELS

The Secret of Terror Castle
The Mystery of the Stuttering Parrot
The Mystery of the Whispering Mummy
The Mystery of the Green Ghost
The Mystery of the Vanishing Treasure
The Secret of Skeleton Island
The Mystery of the Fiery Eye
The Mystery of the Silver Spider
The Mystery of the Screaming Clock
The Mystery of the Moaning Cave
The Mystery of the Talking Skull
The Mystery of the Laughing Shadow
The Secret of the Crooked Cat
The Mystery of the Coughing Dragon
The Mystery of the Flaming Footprints
The Mystery of the Nervous Lion
The Mystery of the Singing Serpent
The Mystery of the Shrinking House
The Secret of Phantom Lake
The Mystery of Monster Mountain
The Secret of the Haunted Mirror
The Mystery of the Dead Man's Riddle
The Mystery of the Invisible Dog
The Mystery of Death Trap Mine
The Mystery of the Dancing Devil
The Mystery of the Headless Horse
The Mystery of the Magic Circle
The Mystery of the Deadly Double
The Mystery of the Sinister Scarecrow
The Secret of Shark Reef
The Mystery of the Scar-Faced Beggar
The Mystery of the Blazing Cliffs

(*Continued on next page*)

The Mystery of the Purple Pirate
The Mystery of the Wandering Cave Man
The Mystery of the Kidnapped Whale
The Mystery of the Missing Mermaid
The Mystery of the Two-Toed Pigeon
The Mystery of the Smashing Glass
The Mystery of the Trail of Terror
The Mystery of the Rogues' Reunion
The Mystery of the Creep-Show Crooks
The Mystery of Wreckers' Rock

FIND YOUR FATE™ MYSTERIES

The Case of the Weeping Coffin
The Case of the Dancing Dinosaur
The Case of the House of Horrors
The Case of the Savage Statue

PUZZLE BOOKS

The Three Investigators' Book of Mystery Puzzles